HUSTLER'S AMBITION

A DUNN FAMILY NOVELLA

THE DUNN FAMILY SERIES

RICKY BLACK

INTRODUCTION

Thanks for checking out Hustler's Ambition! This is the latest in the Dunn Family series and for understanding, is best read alongside Good Deed, Bad Deeds, as the events of this novella directly overlap that book, adding more context and details, as well as new character points of view.

Click here to order if you haven't already, or want to.

-Ricky

CHAPTER ONE
MAY 2020

CAMERON GREENE STARED at his phone screen, ignoring the thumping rap music playing from a dock, the weed stench permeating the room. He hunched further over the phone, refreshing the page at regular intervals. After what seemed like an age, his bet disappeared from the screen. Heart racing, Cameron checked his settled bets, noting his horse had *placed*, but hadn't won.

'Fuck!'

Cameron slammed down his phone, breathing hard. He poured himself a drink from the brandy bottle on his coffee table, stewing over the missed opportunity.

Downing his drink, Cameron grabbed his phone and called a number.

'Yes, Cam. Everything good,' an airy voice answered.

'That tip you gave me was shit,' Cameron snarled. 'What the hell are you playing at?'

'Yo, you begged me for that tip,' the man replied, his tone instantly defensive.

'Whatever. You better come correct next time, or I'm gonna smack you up,' Cameron warned, before hanging up, still fuming over the situation. The winnings would have netted him eight thousand pounds, which would have enabled him to buy the watch he'd had his eye on for a while. Navigating back to the gambling app, he considered putting money on another bet, but hesitated.

Cameron didn't place bets at the same level as some of his associates. Every Friday, it seemed they were at the bookies, or making WhatsApp groups to trade bets. He'd had a few wins, though, and it always seemed like a viable way out. Cameron didn't think he was an addict — quite the contrary. He saw gambling as his answer to investing. Spence had mentioned it to him over the years, emphasising a long-term plan and being prepared for the future. Cameron disagreed. As far as he was concerned, investing and gambling were the same. The only difference was, gambling returned on his investment immediately.

Spence was one of his two best friends, both of whom he worked with. They primarily sold drugs, but had their hands in numerous nefarious ventures.

In their crew, everyone seemed to have a function. Natty Deeds was the ringleader. He ran their small sub-crew. Unquestionably talented, but highly connected, Natty was the nephew of the organisation's boss, Mitch Dunn. Cameron had been lucky to be hired, and was sure he wouldn't have a job if Natty wasn't Mitch's nephew.

It galled him at times. Cameron's friends always seemed to have money, yet he was living week to week, barely staying ahead. Despite their closeness, he couldn't help looking at his friends sceptically sometimes, wondering if he was being paid fairly and whether he could do anything about it if he wasn't.

Cameron's thoughts deepened. He didn't have the same connections as his friends, which left him feeling like he was playing catch up. Natty and Spence had been brought up around crime, moulded and shaped into useful parts of the machine. Natty had his uncle and his dad, and Spence's story was similar. All deep in the life, they could impart their knowledge and wisdom to those next in line.

Cameron didn't have that benefit. Beyond knowing his name, there was little he knew about his father. He'd left nothing to help Cameron learn and grow. Much of what he had learnt, he'd taken from his friends. Leaning on their expertise was uncomfortable for Cameron. He was behind in the game, and that frustrated him.

'Fuck it,' he mumbled, wiping his mouth. He would sleep on it, and sort out his problems tomorrow.

THE FOLLOWING DAY, Cameron woke up, still annoyed about the loss. He'd had to talk himself out of tracking down *Skinny Dave*, the man who had given him the tip. Cameron had won a few bets using his tips in the past, but mostly when backing the clear favourite.

Cameron wondered how connected *Skinny Dave* was. With each bet, Cameron got the increasing impression he was banking on a loser who was trying to get lucky.

Cameron checked the balance on his online banking app, scowling. He glanced around his living room as he ate breakfast, wondering if he had any money around the house. He scratched his chin as he cast his mind back. In his line of work, holding cash was a necessity. It avoided attracting suspicions and unwanted questions. But he doubted there was any he had forgotten about. He was regularly raiding his coffers for clothes and nights out. With a deep sigh, he realised he would have to find other ways to make his money back.

Hustling drugs on the side was a no-go. Their organisation was deep in the streets, and the consequences of getting caught weren't worth it.

Skills-wise, Cameron wasn't the sharpest, especially when

he compared himself to his friends. What he did have was nerve. He was willing to do whatever it took to get to the top of the street crime pile.

After finishing his breakfast, he lit a spliff, still working out how to set things off. His initial instincts were to speak to Natty.

But was it worth involving him?

Natty was sharp and well-respected, with many of the same vices Cameron had. He brought a lot to the table, and Cameron could see the pair running the streets together.

Spence . .

Spence was different. Cameron respected his dad, who he knew was a madman back in the day, but Spence wasn't the same. He was a thinker who read for fun. But worst of all was his natural charm. It had a way of pulling people in and rubbing off on people. Natty was an example of this. Being around Spence had changed him.

In Cameron's eyes, it had made him softer.

Robberies were another option to consider. They were a useful way to make money, but Natty always advised against them. In his eyes, it was a show of desperation. Cameron couldn't see how. He wondered whether these were more *words of wisdom* Natty had taken from Spence, but it was something he felt strongly about.

SOMETIME LATER, Cameron hit the streets, stopping by his crew's main hangout spot. Natty was already there, talking on the phone when Cameron entered. He nodded at Cameron, continuing his call.

'Yes, Cam,' said Carlton. 'You good?'

'What's happening, you little punk?' Cameron replied, grinning as he grabbed the younger man and put him in a headlock. 'What have I told you about staying ready? People aren't messing around on the roads,' he taunted, enjoying seeing Carlton struggle. He was a good kid, but Cameron remembered how he used to run around after Natty, begging to tag along. Natty had taken pity on him and given him a shot, but that didn't mean Cameron had to.

'Leave him alone, Cam,' said Natty. Evidently, he'd finished his call.

'Fine,' snorted Cameron, letting Carlton go. Carlton rubbed his neck, glaring. Cameron considered giving him a slap, but didn't want to hear Natty's shit. He took a seat near Natty, and Carlton left the room.

Their spot was a house that had once belonged to a punter. They'd hung around for years, giving drugs to the owner. They now resided at another place, and Natty and the others threw him a bit of money and product, and took care of the bills. The living room had light blue walls, the paint peeling in places. It had dark blue furniture, and an entertainment system, but not much else in the way of amenities.

'Why are you always defending that little shit?' Cameron asked, glaring at Natty. Natty was an imposing figure. He stood over 6 feet tall, with a muscular build. He had a look that made people take him seriously, but could be strangely charming. Cameron's glare deepened.

'He's a good dude, and he works hard. I don't know why you're always getting at him, but there's no need for it,' said Natty.

'Whatever. It's tough out there, fam. We both know it. I'm just trying to toughen him up.'

'Carlton's not soft. You don't need to worry about him.'

'Fine. Forget him,' said Cameron. 'What's going on?'

Natty shrugged, smoothing the creases in his grey designer sweater.

'Steady day. Spence is working later, but no issues so far. The packs are selling nicely. We've got a reload coming in later. You mind handling it if I'm not around?'

'Yeah, that's calm,' replied Cameron. 'I need to hit a lick or summat, though. My funds are low.'

Natty shot his friend a look. 'If you're broke, I can help you out.'

'I didn't say I was broke,' said Cameron, narrowing his eyes. 'I just want more money.'

'You should talk to Spence. You know he's doing well with his invest—'

'I don't have time to talk to him,' Cameron interjected. 'He's probably with that little slut of his, anyway.'

Natty shook his head, but didn't respond as Carlton re-entered. Cameron glared at his friend again, annoyed by his lack of response. Rising to his feet, Natty made his way to the door, stopping just before it. Turning around and surveying the room, his face contorted.

'This place is a shit-hole. Can you guys give it the once over?' he asked, opening the door and exiting.

Cameron snickered, pushing off from the seat with his hands and standing. After a long stretch, he made his way to the door.

'Yo Cam,' Carlton called out, 'Natty told us to tidy the place up.'

Cameron turned around and impaled Carlton with a glare.

'So fucking tidy it up then,' he replied, slamming the door as he left the room.

―――

CAMERON PUT ASIDE his annoyance with his friends and focused on business. He held the main 'trap phone', directing sales to different places. It was easy enough for him to handle on autopilot, giving him plenty of time to consider his moneymaking options. What he needed were more connections. They would enable him to spread out and diversify his opportunities for earning.

But how he would make those connections, he wasn't sure.

Messing around on his personal phone, he made a few phone calls, trading gossip and little titbits with associates. He received nothing of value, but learnt of a party in the Hood.

———

Cameron was inspecting the contents of his wardrobe later that day. Rifling through it, he selected his clothes, laying them on his bed. Picking up his phone, he navigated to his contacts and called Natty.

'Yes, Cam. What's happening, bro?'

'I've got a party for us later. Meant to be bare women there. Are you on it?'

Cameron heard Natty's yawn, and frowned, sure his friend would decline.

'Yeah, why not? If it's dead or there's no women around, I'm blaming you, though. Send me the details. I'll drag Spence along too. Cool?'

'Cool.' Cameron didn't think Spence would come, but it didn't matter either way. 'I'll send you a text with the details. Come to my yard tonight, and we can fly over there together.'

'Cool,' replied Natty, hanging up.

Cameron rubbed his hands together, grinning. He needed to cut loose, and the party sounded like the perfect way to do it.

CHAPTER TWO

CAMERON GRINNED as he entered the party, flanked by Natty and Spence. His grin faded when he saw people flock to Natty, touching his fist and engaging him in conversation, but he put it aside, determined to enjoy the night. He made a beeline for a table laden with drinks, fixing himself a brandy and coke. Spence followed, making his own drink as he surveyed the room in front of him.

Cameron didn't know how many people had initially been invited, but the house was packed. Though he'd recognised the address, he didn't know who the host was, but imagined they wouldn't be pleased with the number of people in the spot. As he thought this, he heard the sound of something smashing, followed by loud voices. Cameron grinned, knowing the owner would be pissed that things had been broken.

Spence nodded his head to the music, which surprised Cameron, as he'd never expressed an interest in any drill songs. Deciding it wasn't important, he finished his drink and made another, feeling Spence's eyes on him.

'What?' He said, cutting his eyes to his friend. 'It's a party.'

Spence shrugged, but Cameron noted the judgement in his eyes. Before he could say anything else, Natty sauntered over with a smirk on his face.

'You definitely came through on the women front,' he told Cameron. 'Danny's been here an hour and has already got a gobble from some random girl.'

Spence made a face. 'Lucky guy.'

'Does your girl not give blowies?' Cameron snarked, knowing full well that she did. Unbeknownst to his friend, he had been involved with Spence's girlfriend Anika a few years ago, and knew precisely what she was and wasn't into.

Spence rolled his eyes. 'Here we go. Wouldn't be a night out without you finding some way to mention my girlfriend.'

'Nope.' Natty shook his head, making fresh drinks for everyone. 'We're not doing this tonight. We're here to have a good time. That's what we're going to do. Everyone drink up, and let's be happy.'

Spence and Cameron took the drinks, and the trio downed them. Natty thumped his chest, grinning.

'There we go! Let's get it popping in here.'

AND, so they did. Cameron lost track of the number of drinks he'd consumed. They did the rounds, drinking, partaking in smoking various joints that were going around. Cameron even did a few lines, then danced with fuzzy women that he struggled to recall. He didn't know when he left the party, or how he got home, but he awoke the next day in bed, to someone banging on his door.

Finally, he answered, letting Natty in.

'You look horrific,' said Natty, sounding spry, and much fresher than Cameron felt. Taking pity, Natty made them both cups of coffee, which they sat outside and drank. The hot drink made Cameron feel a little better, which he was thankful for. Despite feeling rough, he was glad he'd gone to the party. It had taken his mind off things, and he'd had a great time.

As the pair sat there, Cameron learned Natty had ended up at Lorraine's place. Their situation was a strange one. Natty had been on and off with her for years. In that time, she'd managed to have a child with another guy . . . Raider, a rival hustler and enemy of Natty's. Stranger still, Natty spent more time around Lorraine and her son than Raider did. Cameron didn't get it, but felt Natty was loved up, even if his friend would never admit it.

Cameron couldn't understand, and didn't think he ever would. Natty owed Lorraine nothing, yet remained a presence in her life. He grew angry at Cameron when he teased him about the relationship, but he'd put himself in that position.

Cameron put it to one side, and after finishing their drinks, his mind skipped back to Spence.

'I still feel rough,' he moaned, yawning as he put on a pair of trainers. 'Seriously, how long are we gonna let him get away with that?'

'What are you talking about?' Natty asked, frowning.

'Anika. You said in the beginning that she wouldn't change him, and I told you he was pussy whipped. Now look at him . . . leaving parties early when we're having a good time so he can run back to her.'

'They live together now. Spence does what he thinks is right. You don't know that she's having that kind of effect,' said Natty.

'I know her, remember? We both do.'

Natty shook his head.

'C'mon, let's just go and see the old man.'

That wasn't good enough, Cameron thought, as they headed for Natty's car. What Spence was doing wasn't right. He'd come out with the crew, and unless he hooked up with a girl at the party, he should have left with them. Instead, he'd ducked out early. The most annoying part was that Natty didn't seem to care. He constantly gave Spence a pass over everything, and once Cameron had noticed this, he couldn't stop noticing it. Whenever he opened his mouth, he was perceived as the bad guy.

He knew Anika, though. He knew her better than both Natty and Spence. She was a happy, good-time girl, who he'd pursued with ease, then cut off when she became too clingy. Somehow, she had ended up with Spence. Cameron wasn't sure if she had done it to get back at him, but wouldn't put it past her.

———

NATTY DROVE to Rudy's office on Francis Street, the pair making conversation and listening to music. Cameron's head was pounding, and Natty was handling it in his usual manner, being louder and making his head hurt more.

Soon, they pulled up outside Rudy's. He worked out of a house belonging to an older woman, Delores. Cameron didn't know why, and had never been interested enough to see if Natty knew. They spoke with the guards milling around outside, then headed into the house.

Rudy sat in the kitchen, sipping a drink. Delores was pottering around. As always, she had a smile and words for Natty, yet ignored Cameron. He glanced at Rudy, hoping the older man would look up and take notice of him, but he didn't.

Rudy Campbell was the number two guy in the Dunn organisation. He had short hair, and wore a pristine white shirt, finally glancing up at the pair with his piercing eyes, which, to no surprise, lingered on Natty.

Cameron didn't pay much attention to the conversation. Instead, he studied the way the pair spoke to one another.

HUSTLER'S AMBITION

Even with Natty's last name, and his status as Mitch Dunn's nephew, Rudy still outranked him by a considerable margin. The fact he was sleeping with Natty's mum also played into their relationship, which always seemed laced with tension.

Cameron spaced out for a moment, sure he wouldn't be involved in the conversation. His attention returned sharply when Natty mentioned *Elijah*. Cameron focused on the back of his friend's head as he spoke.

Elijah was a rival dealer who they didn't get along with. There had been tension between the crews for a while, and Natty was one of the most outspoken against them. But Natty lacked the objectivity to make a sound assessment. Lorraine's ex-boyfriend, Raider, worked for Elijah. It made it difficult to separate Natty's true concerns from his personal agenda.

Still exhausted from his late night, Cameron yawned, just as Rudy looked in his direction. Cameron froze, but Rudy had already focused on Natty again, making Cameron feel like he'd missed an opportunity to establish himself.

They didn't stay much longer, and Cameron's annoyance only grew as they headed back to Natty's car. Rudy had paid him little attention, and hadn't said a word to him. If he was ever going to ascend to the level he wanted, that needed to change.

'No point in me even going,' Cameron grumbled when Natty drove away. 'Rudy didn't even speak to me. Old prick.'

Natty didn't respond, lost in thought as he drove. Cameron scowled.

'Natty? What are you thinking about?'

'Elijah,' said Natty.

'What about him?'

'I don't trust him,' replied Natty. Cameron almost rolled his eyes.

Here we go again, he thought.

'Him or Raider? You sure the fact your fuckpiece's ex rolls with him isn't clouding your judgement?'

'I'm sure. This is business,' snapped Natty. The conversation continued, but Cameron wasn't sure he believed him. Natty seemed different lately. Even when they went out, it felt like he was going through the motions at times, and Cameron was sure it was due to Lorraine.

If it wasn't him, it was Spence, loved up with his girlfriend. He didn't understand what was happening to his crew, making him wonder if he was the one with the problem.

Anika had fallen hard for him, he'd recognised that. She'd wanted a commitment, and he'd just wanted to sleep with her, and see her when it was convenient.

So, he broke it off

And then one night, at a club, he'd watched from afar as she and Spence began talking — Natty stepping in and stopping him from intervening.

Now, a year later, they were still together, and Cameron hated it. It wasn't that he regretted his actions with Anika, or that he thought he'd missed his chance. He didn't want Anika, but he didn't want his friend to have her either.

'Don't overthink it, bro,' Cameron responded to a comment Natty had made about Rudy's judgement in potentially working with Elijah. 'Have the meeting, get shit organised, and keep it moving. We can get put on in a major way, and trust me, I need that.' He thought about the money he'd lost betting, and the money he'd blown on other things.

He needed to make it back, and then some.

CHAPTER THREE

AFTER LEAVING NATTY, Cameron mooched around for a while. In the evening, he stopped by Philip's place. Philip was an old acquaintance from back in the day. He was game for a laugh and always had good weed. They were getting high, when Cameron remembered his earlier thoughts.

'I need money, Phil,' he said, handing his friend the spliff.

'Money's easy to come by,' Philip bragged, inhaling the joint, ignoring the fact he lived in a grotty bedsit. 'I know loads of people making serious money. If I had the startup funds, I'd be right there with them.'

'What are they doing?' Cameron asked, intrigued.

'All that crypto stuff mainly. It's easy. They stick their money in, hold for a bit, and make pure profit,' said Philip. He spoke for a while about the setup, but Cameron had heard enough. All he cared about were the potential profits. He'd heard people mention cryptocurrency before, but it all sounded too technical for him. *If he had a way in, he'd be a fool not to take it*, he mused.

'Are you interested?' Philip asked. 'I can give you Lodi's number if you like.'

'Yeah, I'm on it,' said Cameron, grinning. Philip shot him a look.

'Just . . . be careful, bro. Crypto is no joke. People get ripped off when they don't know what they're doing.'

'I'll be fine,' said Cameron, airily waving his hand. 'Stop hogging the zoot.'

A FEW DAYS LATER, Cameron met Lodi. He was a tall, mixed-raced man with glasses, a diamond earring, and an easy demeanour. Cameron surveyed the man, impressed by Lodi's designer warm-up suit. He wondered if the rest of his wardrobe was as impressive.

Cameron allowed himself a moment to think about his future. This man was going to make him rich, and that would change his life in the best possible way.

'Phil told me about you,' said Lodi, turning down the music. They were sat in his car, parked on Louis Street. Even as Cameron sat in the passenger seat, he was aware of a group of kids staring at the pair. He shot one of them a hard look, and the group hurried on. 'He said you're interested in making some real money.'

'Always,' said Cameron. 'Only if it's for real, though. I'm not trying to get messed around.'

Lodi nodded.

'Course not, fam. Phil was crystal clear. I know who you're down with. You're a real guy.'

Cameron grinned, all but pushing his chest out. He liked when he received the respect he thought he deserved; the respect that should come with being a member of the Dunn organisation.

'Good. I'm glad you recognise. So, how can you help me get rich?'

Lodi smoothly went into a speech about how he made his

money, offering to invest money on Cameron's behalf. The profits were regular and plentiful; he had messages and photos on his phone, testimonials from all the successful transactions he'd made, and the people he'd helped.

'What's in it for you?' Cameron asked, eyes narrowed. It all sounded too good to be true, and he was wary about being ripped off.

'I get five percent of your profits. Sounds like a lot, but you won't even notice it after you go around a few times.' Phil paused for a moment. 'I know it's a big risk, so why don't we do a small deal to establish trust?'

'How small?' Cameron asked.

'It's up to you. Whatever you want to risk, I'll make it work. Let's say no lower than two hundred and fifty quid.'

Cameron mulled it over, deciding it was worth the risk. This was his chance to establish himself. He reached into his pocket and counted out the money, handing it to Lodi.

'Don't play with me,' he warned. Lodi grinned.

'Course not, bro. I'll be in touch.'

CAMERON WENT ABOUT HIS BUSINESS, not expecting to see Lodi for a while. It was a shock when three days later, Lodi called, eagerly wanting to meet.

'Here you go,' he said, as soon as Cameron climbed into his car. 'This is your profit.'

Cameron's mouth fell open when he took the stack of money from Lodi. He'd hoped the man was on the level, but he was still shocked to see what he had achieved in such a short amount of time.

'How much is here?' He asked, fingering the notes. 'Looks like a grand.'

Lodi nodded, grinning.

'Yeah, man. Four times profit on your first go-around. You got in at the right time.'

Cameron couldn't stop looking at the money. He'd held larger amounts in his hands, but the fact it had come so easily was intoxicating. He'd handed over his money with little expectation, but the outcome was astonishing. As he sat staring at the cash in his hands, a single thought occurred; *the more I invest, the more I will earn.*

The idea of lording it in Spence's face that he was a better investor propelled him. Still holding the money, he faced Lodi.

'I wanna go again.'

Lodi's eyes widened. 'Already? Don't you want to spend what you made?'

Cameron swiftly shook his head.

'I'm serious about this moneymaking shit,' he said. 'Take this grand, and I'll get you another grand ASAP.'

Lodi looked away. Cameron's eyes narrowed.

'What? Why are you acting like that?'

'Because . . .' Lodi took a deep breath. 'Look, I've got something serious I can let you in on . . . but this is top-level shit. Makes this look like nothing.' He held up the bundle of notes in his hand.

'I want in on it,' said Cameron instantly.

'Cam . . . it's a minimum of five grand,' said Lodi quietly. 'I can take this grand as a down payment, but I'll need another four thousand by the end of the week if you're serious.'

Cameron's stomach plummeted. Five thousand was a considerable commitment. He had some money put down, but it wouldn't be enough.

He couldn't afford to miss out on this opportunity, though.

'What sort of return would we be looking at?'

Lodi didn't reply immediately. He studied Cameron for so long that Cameron grew annoyed.

'Oi! Are you listening?'

'I want to make sure you're serious. Risk high, win high . . . Cam . . . that's my motto. Don't let my shitty car fool you. I'm stacking. I do these deals all the time. If you go in on this, you're looking at thirty, forty grand.'

That sealed it for Cameron; the idea of making so much money in one sitting too much to overcome.

'You'll have your money.'

———

GIDDY at the thought of profiting, Cameron managed to scrape together four thousand pounds. He had to borrow some from his mum, had some luck winning on online roulette, and borrowed one thousand pounds from another street associate. Handing the money to Lodi, he sat back, beaming, imagining holding the returns in his hands. Being able to lord it over his friends was another bonus. They were constantly trying to push investment advice on him. Criticising him for how he spent his money. The thought of proving he was the most astute investor of the three thrilled him.

Lodi took the money, promising he would be in touch, and Cameron went about his business, waiting for a call.

After three days, he'd heard nothing. Lodi hadn't said how long it would take, but based on the last turnaround, he'd expected to hear something.

At home one night, he called Lodi, having built and lit a spliff. He inhaled the potent weed, waiting for Lodi to answer.

The phone just kept ringing.

Panicking, Cameron tried several more times, but the

result was the same. He left text messages, and thinking Lodi could have been asleep, he tried again the next day.

The result was the same. Lodi wasn't answering the phone. Cameron's panic only grew as he realised he knew little about the man. He didn't know where he lived, or where he hung out . . . only the car he drove.

Cameron drove to Philip's house, banging on the door until Philip answered.

'Cam, what the hell, man? It's nearly midnight.' Philip yawned as he opened the door. Cameron pushed past him, dragging him into the house and shoving him into the living room. 'What the fuck are you doing?'

'Where's your boy?'

'Which boy? What are you talking about?'

Cameron shook his head, grabbing Philip by the scruff of his t-shirt.

'Don't play with me. Where's Lodi?' he snarled.

'I don't know, mate! I put you two together, but I don't know where he stays.'

'Convenient, isn't it . . .' Cameron growled. 'I'm after a payday, and you know just the guy to help me, then he rips me off? Do you think I'm a dickhead?'

'Cam, listen, I don't know anything about it. I swear.' Philip's eyes were wide as he trembled with fear. None of it made Cameron feel any better. All he could think about was the five thousand pounds he'd foolishly given a man he didn't know.

'Shut up!' He snarled, overcome with rage. He drove his fist into Philip's stomach. Philip was a talker. He wasn't a fighter, and he instantly folded, gasping in pain. Cameron hit him again, shoving him to the floor, kicking him repeatedly, not wanting to stop.

Ignoring the screams of the man he'd hung his hopes on, Cameron continued to drive the air out of him, wanting to see the light in his eyes extinguished.

Breathing hard, he stopped kicking, glaring down at the man who had curled up into a ball.

'I'm not playing, Phil. Your boy fucked with the wrong one. Either he or you owes me five grand. If I don't get it, you're dead, and then I'll track him down.' Cameron grabbed Philip, pulling him to his feet and ignoring his whimpering. 'You know which crew I'm down with, and you know how we handle shit. I want my money, or else.'

Shoving Philip onto the sofa, Cameron stormed from the house, leaving a sobbing Philip in his wake.

CHAPTER FOUR

RUDY CAMPBELL GLANCED at his coffee cup, then up at Elijah. The pair were at a coffee shop in Roundhay, out of the mix and away from prying eyes.

'We need to go to the pub next time,' Rudy grumbled, taking a sip of coffee that burnt his mouth. Elijah smirked.

'I like this environment. It's quiet for the most part, if you know when to come.'

'You just want to be Teflon,' Rudy teased him. Elijah chuckled.

'He did alright in our game,' he pointed out. Rudy couldn't disagree. He had worked for Mitch Dunn for over twenty years. He had direct access to almost all the organisation's resources, relative freedom to make decisions and had amassed extraordinary wealth. He was the undisputed number two, but despite his success, he remained frustrated.

As the years progressed, Rudy had seen a change in Mitch Dunn. Where success made Rudy hungry for more, he felt it had softened Mitch; allowing him to fade into the background in contentedness. Rudy believed his boss was out of touch and out of practice.

Teflon was a prime example of what hunger, desire and

timing could achieve. He had always worked for himself, building up his drug firm until it sat head and shoulders above the competition.

Rudy longed for that power; a legacy he could look back on with pride.

Though younger, Elijah was a powerful, respected dealer in his own right. He was known as one of the *smart breed* — a term used to describe the drug dealers who focused on business. Consequently, Elijah had done well, and had been nipping at the heels of the Dunns for the past few years.

Rudy had realised Elijah and his infrastructure could be the push needed to remove Mitch from power. They had been feeling one another out for months, but were beginning to make progress.

'Where are we at?' Elijah continued after a minute.

'I spoke with Mitch. He's okayed the move in Little London.'

'How did he take it?' Elijah leant forward, intrigued.

Rudy shrugged. 'He doesn't care as long as it makes money. It ties into what I've been saying for a while. He's lost his edge, and he's no longer looking at all the angles.'

'Go on . . .'

'He doesn't wonder why I'd want to set up shop in Little London all of a sudden. I don't think he even cares. We've never tried to do it before, and for good reason. Our profits are still up. We run a tight ship, and everyone knows that. Extending our arm into another area risks spreading ourselves too thin. Not only does it risk failure in Little London, but it presents opportunity for other organisations within our current areas. It's a risk that any boss engaged with their business would consider thoroughly.'

'Maybe he just trusts your judgement and that you've done your due diligence. You've been working with him for years. A concentrated and effective expansion means more profit. That's more money in your pocket and his.' Elijah's eyebrow rose as he looked across at Rudy, his nostrils flaring and his head shaking.

'He's out of touch,' Rudy concluded. Elijah took another sip of his drink.

'Do we take him out now then?'

Rudy scratched his chin.

'We need to keep moving slowly. I've got access to most of the higher-ups in the firm, but I'm still working out who can be trusted.'

Elijah nodded, satisfied with the response.

'Moving onto Little London then. Who's gonna lead it?'

'Nathaniel is the only logical choice,' said Rudy.

'Natty's a wildcard, Rudy. Wonder is a solid choice. Natty's too stubborn to play ball,' said Elijah.

'Think long-term,' Rudy started, lowering his voice when a staff member grabbed some empty cups from a nearby table. 'Nathaniel could be a key play in this movement. I've suggested this to you before. Add to that he's frustrated with his position. I can twist that in our favour. Somebody as emotional as him is easily manipulated. He wants reassurance. He wants guidance. But above all, he wants agreement. Nathaniel believes he's ready to ascend and that his uncle is actively blocking him. We need to lean into that.'

'Get him to resent his uncle?' Elijah questioned. Rudy nodded, a sinister grin on his face.

'Having Mitch's nephew on board *would* be a great move,' Elijah admitted — albeit grudgingly. 'If he doesn't work out, though, we're replacing him.'

Rudy didn't like how Elijah had put that to him, but it wasn't worth expanding on at this stage.

'Fair enough. Depending how things go, there's a chance we can bring Nathaniel in on our vision. He's hungry, and he's looking for opportunity. We're all looking for opportunity. That's why we're here.'

'I get it,' said Elijah. 'I guess we'll arrange another meeting soon, once there are more developments.'

Elijah touched Rudy's fist, then left. Rudy hung back, finishing his drink, evaluating the meeting he'd just had. Elijah was sharp, pragmatic, but potentially too switched on for his own good. Rudy would need to keep an eye on him. He had worked too hard and put up with too much, to have anyone get in the way of his end goals.

CHAPTER FIVE

CAMERON QUICKENED his step as he hurried to Philip's place. Leaving the gate open, he hammered on the door until Philip answered, his posture stooped.

'Move out the way,' Cameron told him, inwardly grinning when Philip did as he was told. 'What do you have for me?' He asked, when they were stood in Philip's living room. Sighing, Philip rummaged in a nearby drawer and handed Cameron a stack of money.

'There's eight hundred quid there. It's all I could get this week,' said Philip. Cameron stuffed the money in his pocket, sizing Philip up.

'Have you heard from your boy yet?'

Philip shook his head. 'I haven't seen him in weeks. I swear down.'

'For your sake, I hope you're still telling the truth,' Cameron warned. 'Natty and his uncle aren't happy with you. They're leaving it to me for now, but if you carry on fucking around, you're finished.'

Philip trembled with fear, and Cameron loved it. He was lying to him about Natty and his uncle. They didn't know about him getting ripped off, and he intended to keep it that way. Using their name had paid off, though, and for the past few weeks, he'd collected three thousand pounds from Philip. He didn't know how he was getting the money, nor did he care, as long he got paid.

'I'll be back next week. Make sure you've got summat, and if Lodi dares show his face, I'd better hear from you.'

Cameron left Philip's place, grinning as he heard the man sobbing before he closed the door. He didn't care about his plight. As far as he was concerned, Philip was complicit in setting him up, or was too stupid to verify Lodi before making the introduction. Either way, Cameron didn't intend to lose out.

He hoped Lodi did resurface, already planning how he would take care of him if he did. Whatever he decided to do, he planned on making it as painful as he could manage.

He'd reached home when his phone rang. Grumbling to himself when he saw the caller, he answered.

'Hey, mum. What's up?'

'Hey, Cam. Are there any letters at the house for me?'

'One came for you this morning. Looks like junk, though. I'll drop it around tomorrow.'

'Okay, thank you. I'm expecting an important letter, and I'm worried they'll still have that address. What about the other thing?'

Cameron frowned. 'What other thing?'

'The money I lent you. When are you paying it back?'

'I'm working on it,' replied Cameron, knowing he had the money to pay her back in his pocket. His mum sighed.

'That's not good enough, Cam. I went without to lend you that money, and you promised to pay me back weeks ago.'

'I'm working on it, I told you,' snapped Cameron. 'What's the matter? Your hubby mad that you lent your son some money? Is he still trying to pretend I don't exist?'

'Grow up, Cameron. This isn't about my partner. This is about you not sticking to your commitments. Don't you think there's something wrong with still needing to borrow money from me?'

'I'm not doing this with you. Like I said, I'll pay you back when I can. You can collect this letter when you like. Turns out I'm busy tomorrow,' he said, hanging up. He tossed the phone aside, furious at his mum. He was her only son, and she still felt the need to run him down for money like he was a stranger.

For the longest time, she had put her new life ahead of him. Cameron recalled doing his share around the house, and helping her with the bills when she was struggling. She had moved in with her long-term partner a few years ago, leaving Cameron in charge of the house.

Like many people in his life, she had a selective memory.

Putting his annoyance to one side, Cameron counted the money he'd taken from Philip, binding it with an elastic band and putting it in his makeshift hiding place; a compartment in his TV stand.

Taking his phone out, he opened the gambling app, navigating to a race that was due to start shortly. He selected the favourite to win and entered the amount of money he had collected from Philip. His eyes lit up when he saw the potential returns. Blowing out a breath, he forced closed the application.

The majority of the money would go toward paying off the debt he had accrued when he'd gathered money to give to Lodi. He couldn't risk losing it again.

When he'd finished, Cameron had a cigarette and a cup of coffee, then called Natty.

'Cam, what's up? Where you at?'

'Home. I was gonna swing by if you're about.'

'Yeah, fly through. I should be around for a bit.'

Cameron hung up, checked his outfit, then headed to Natty's. When he arrived, Natty was sitting outside, smoking a cigarette. As Cameron approached, one of Natty's neighbours walked by with her dog, giving Natty a wide smile.

'Hello, Nathaniel. It's good to see you out and about. You're looking well,' she said. Cameron was impressed. She was an older woman, with reddish brown hair and curves that her dowdy style of dress couldn't hide.

'Thanks, Deidre,' Natty replied, giving her a pleasant grin. 'Tell Dave I said hi, and that I'll drop the screwdriver off sometime.'

'I'll do that. I'll have a cup of tea ready for you, when you choose to stop by . . .' With a wave, Deidre left them, but not before giving Natty a lingering look.

'Bro, I know you're handling that,' remarked Cameron, watching the woman disappear down the road.

'Nah, she's cool. Her husband's a good dude too. She's just bored and likes to flirt sometimes.'

'She can flirt with me anytime. You're going soft, bro. Lorraine must be inside,' Cameron joked.

'Fuck you. Fuck Lorraine too,' said Natty, scowling. Cameron was surprised he and Lorraine were still on the outs. Natty had grumbled about it to Spence a few days ago, but Cameron hadn't paid much attention.

'Whatever. What are you up to, anyway?'

'Nothing much. Got a meeting, then I need to go and see Rudy. Just killing time until then.'

'Who are you meeting with?'

'Don't worry about it. It's not important,' Natty replied. Cameron's eyes narrowed.

'Not like you to be keeping secrets, fam.'

'Not everything is for everyone to know. It's not that deep,' said Natty. Cameron shrugged. If it was important, he was sure he would find out later.

'Fine. Listen, speak to Rudy for me. Let him know what I can do. Our team needs to step up, fam. I mean, I wanna enter my thirties with proper money behind me . . . know what I mean?'

Natty sighed, flicking away his unfinished cigarette.

'I know. I want more too. Life is just flying by, and I feel like I haven't made a dent yet. Even Jaden; he's getting older. I still remember him as a baby, but he's only a few years off being a teenager. It's mad.'

'I get you,' said Cameron, though he didn't. He couldn't fathom why Jaden would be a factor in Natty's mindset. The messy situation made his head hurt.

'I want more control over the things I'm doing. I've been doing this forever, and things are always the same,' Natty continued. 'I want to feel like I'm actually taking a step forward.'

Cameron lit a cigarette of his own, borrowing Natty's lighter and handing it back to his friend.

'You're in a better position than most, though, fam,' he said. 'I mean, you're *Hood royalty*.'

Natty snorted, shooting Cameron a disparaging look.

'I don't get treated like I'm *Hood royalty*, do I? I'm just another worker to my uncle.'

'If that's the case, you definitely need to keep Rudy sweet,' said Cameron. 'He's the key to us stepping up. You know him better than I do. How can I make him see me as an asset? *Us* as assets?'

Natty didn't respond immediately. He had a sulky look on his face that Cameron understood, but ignored. It wasn't the time for Natty to get emotional.

'Rudy is just Rudy. He's always been around. You know that. There's not much I can tell you about him. He's like my uncle; he likes things quiet, and wants things in order.'

'Fair enough,' said Cameron, already mulling over how he could get onto Rudy's radar. A brainwave struck him. 'What about Marlon?'

'What about him?' Natty's tone grew cold. Marlon worked for Rudy, and was definitely someone Rudy kept close.

'He might be another good guy to know,' explained Cameron.

'He's a little arse-licker. He can't do shit for us.'

Cameron let it go. He was aware of the dislike between the pair, wondering if Natty was letting his dislike for people stand in the way of their progress. It was something that required more thought.

'You wanna go get a drink when you're done with your meetings?'

'Yeah, I could do with a distraction,' said Natty. 'I'll bell you when I'm finished, and stop by your place.'

'You sure you can make it?' Cameron teased. 'Don't you need to ask Lorraine's permission?'

'Don't make me smack you.'

CHAPTER SIX

THAT NIGHT, the pair had a few drinks at Cameron's before hitting the city centre, finding a spot just off Briggate. It was a rougher bar, where some of the Hood guys liked to hang out. The music was harder, and as they entered, the usual deadly vibe was in the air. The pair were equal to it, meeting the hard eyes of various people as they made their way through the venue.

Cameron wondered what Spence would have thought of the place. In all likelihood, they would have struggled to get him through the door.

They ordered drinks, and after three brandies and cokes, Cameron was already feeling it, enjoying the buzz he had going. After another drink, he was in the bathroom, throwing up, thankful none of it had got on his clothes.

Gargling some water, he paid for some mouthwash from the bathroom attendant, then sorted himself out before heading back out to the bar. Immediately, he spotted a leggy, brown-skinned girl that reminded him of Anika. His jaw tightened, but it surprised Cameron that she'd registered with him. She was drinking with a group of girls, none of whom Cameron recognised.

Shelving it, he headed back to Natty, who was talking to a burly man in an ill-fitting Moncler hooded top. He moved away just as Cameron approached.

'Who was that?' He asked.

'Some dude who knows my family,' said Natty. 'You feeling better? Need any water or anything?' He asked in a mock-concerned voice.

'I'm good. Might need to slow down for a min, though. Listen, I've seen one that I want. Need you to keep the friends distracted while I move to her.'

Natty shrugged, and they headed over. Cameron chuckled as Natty immediately drew the attention of the brown-skinned girl's friends. Cameron approached with a smirk on his face.

'What are you saying?' He asked the girl. She glanced at her friends, then back to him. 'What do they call you, beautiful?'

'Whitney,' she said after a moment, Cameron barely able to hear her soft voice over the music. He bought her a drink, and learned a little more about her. Whitney was twenty-three and went to university. She seemed nervous at first, but seemed to warm up to Cameron after a while, and he eventually led her outside.

As they smoked a cigarette, he was about to go in for the kill, when a loud voice interrupted them.

'Oi, what's going on here?'

'Shit,' Whitney mumbled. Cameron shot her a questioning look as a man strode over to them, flanked by several other guys. He wore a black shirt and jeans, standing a few inches taller than Cameron with a furious look on his face. After scowling at Cameron, the man turned to Whitney.

'What the hell are you doing out? You told me you had work to do,' he snarled.

'I was taking a break,' stammered Whitney. 'I wasn't doing anything, babe. Honest.'

'*Babe?*' Cameron repeated. 'Is this your man?'

The man stepped closer to Cameron.

'Don't worry about who I am. Stay away from my girl, or else.'

'Yeah? Or else what?' Cameron didn't back down. Before the man could say anything else, Natty and the other girls spilled out of the club. Natty took in the scene in an instant, stepping to Cameron's side.

'What's going on here?' He said. The other men all looked at one another. Natty's presence had changed things. He was bigger than any of the men, even if the pair were outnumbered. Already, the man's friends had backed up a step.

'Your mate here was fucking around with my girl.'

'It wasn't like that!' Whitney protested.

'Shut it,' her boyfriend snapped.

'Listen, I don't care what happened. That's my boy you're starting on. I suggest you back off, take your girl, and go.'

'Who the fuck are you to tell me what to do?' The man started on Natty now, whose jaw tightened.

'Oi, take it away from the club,' a pot-bellied bouncer called out. No one listened. Cameron noticed Natty had shifted his feet, slightly angling his body, ready for a fight. The man wasn't listening to reason, and Cameron was done with the drama. Swinging, he caught the man in the side of the face, then hit him again before the man could react.

Chaos ensued. Whitney was screaming. Natty had surged forward, hitting one of the man's friends. Cameron noted the man hitting the ground hard, before a blow stunned him. They heard noises from behind them, quickly turning their attention.

'Nobody move,' the larger of the two police officers yelled as they rushed onto the scene.

With a glance at one another, Natty and Cameron bolted, laughing together as they ran off into the night.

After a few minutes, they stopped, breathing hard, but away from the fray.

'Fucking hell,' said Cameron, buoyed with what had transpired. His cheek smarted from where he had been hit, but Natty had his back, with no issue. 'It's good to know the old Nat is still in there, bro. I appreciate the backup.'

'Always,' said Natty, rubbing his hand. 'What the fuck was that about?'

'Women, fam. They're scandalous. Can you believe she lied to her man about where she was? She didn't even mention having a boyfriend.'

'It wouldn't have stopped you even if she had,' Natty pointed out.

'Yeah, probably not. It's bad, though. You can't trust any of them. I bet Anika is the same, when Spence is with us. You've seen the friends she hangs out with. They're a bunch of slags.'

'Leave it alone,' said Natty, his voice hard. Cameron shrugged, touching his cheek again, hoping it wouldn't bruise. He'd been caught with a nice shot, but was pleased it hadn't dropped him.

'Fine. You wanna call it a night, or do you wanna go somewhere else?'

'I'm off home,' said Natty. 'My hand hurts. Probably best we stay out of trouble for now too. We don't need this town shit getting back to people.'

'Cool,' replied Cameron. After saying their goodbyes, they jumped into separate taxis. When Cameron arrived home, he had a spliff, still chuckling over how the night had transpired. Afterwards, he headed to bed, stuck on a film and fell asleep.

CHAPTER SEVEN

A FEW DAYS LATER, Cameron was leaving Maureen's on Roundhay Road, food in hand, when he noticed Marlon climbing from a car, about to walk in. His pulse raised as he realised this was his opportunity to make an impression.

'Yo, Marlon. You good?'

Marlon glanced up, blinking quizzically when he noticed Cameron.

'*Cam*, right? What's happening?' He finally said.

'Just getting some food.' Cameron motioned to the bag. 'I've been meaning to speak to you for a while.'

'What about?' Marlon frowned. He was a short, wiry man, with short hair, glasses, and a neat beard.

'I'm doing my thing on the blocks, but I want more.' Cameron noted Marlon looking around, panicking as he realised he was losing him. 'I know this ain't the right place to speak about things, but I wanna grow, fam. Just reach out if there's anything I can do.'

'You're Deeds' boy, right?' Marlon's frown only deepened. Cameron understood it. Marlon and Natty had never been on good terms, but things worsened when Natty slept with his girlfriend back in the day. Marlon had been furious when he found out, but his response was limited to a few harsh words. It galled Marlon that Natty was the crew's protected commodity, but he knew the rules.

'Yeah, but don't let that stop shit. Natty is my boy, but I'm my own person. Just gimme a shot to step up,' Cameron pressed. Carefully, Marlon surveyed him, before nodding.

'I'm not promising anything, but we'll see,' he said. 'Anyway, I'm hungry, so I'm gonna go in.' He motioned to the restaurant. Cameron stepped out of the way and headed to his car, hoping he hadn't overplayed his hand. He didn't understand why so many things were getting in his way. Cameron was the last of a dying breed, willing to get down and dirty to make his money, but people didn't seem to care.

Even Lodi had played him.

Cameron's jaw clenched as he drove away. He wondered if Marlon would tell Rudy about him; if word would get back to Natty about his request. Cameron didn't think he was doing anything wrong, but you never knew how things would play out on the streets.

Thinking of Lodi made his stomach churn.

He'd looked forward to flaunting his investments to his friends; to seeing their shocked faces. It appeared increasingly more likely that his friends would see his sombre face, as he asked them for their help.

Cameron's nostrils flared as he imagined Spence talking him through *the basics of investing.* He had tried numerous times, but Cameron had always shut it down. What frustrated him the most was that it never seemed to bother Spence. He took it in his stride, moving on amicably and offering his help *when Cam was ready to listen.* He always seemed to have his things in order: Good position, plenty of money, sound investments and a partner he loved.

Cameron's mind drifted to the girl he had met in the bar, wondering briefly what could have been. He quickly realised that what he'd seen in her was a similarity with a girl he used to be with; Anika.

Ultimately, Cameron wasn't sure what he wanted. It confused and irked him that he'd thought about Anika as much as he had recently.

Lately, everything seemed to irk him. Cameron was sure he wanted to do something; to step up, but everything felt cloudy to him. He couldn't help comparing himself to the moves his friends were making. Spence seemed confident, content in his own lane. *As soft as he was, at least he was happy*, Cameron mused, driving onto Spencer Place.

He wondered if that was Anika's effect on Spence, but struggled to see it. Based on what he knew about her, he couldn't remember many positives about her character, outside of her looks.

Smoking a spliff, he finished his food and had a drink, listening to music on Youtube, wondering how to spend his night. Since his fight in town with Natty, he'd worked the last few days, keeping his head down and grinding. He finally reached for his phone, and called an old link.

'Hey, Cam,' she answered. 'It's been a while.'

'I know. You wanna come over, smoke a spliff and chill?'

'You're shameless,' she replied, laughing. 'Aren't you even going to ask how I am?'

'Course I am. Face to face, though. You know I've always got the good shit,' he bragged, grinning when she giggled.

'You're lucky I'm on a break from my boyfriend.'

'I know I am. Come on over, and I'll scratch that itch for you.'

'Whatever. I'll be over in an hour.'

'Drop me a message. I'll get you an Uber,' Cameron told her.

'You don't have to do that.'

'It's cool. Message me.'

Cameron hung up, then headed to the bathroom. He

showered, throwing on an Arsenal football shirt and a pair of tracksuit bottoms. Maxine knew the drill, and he saw no reason to dress up for her. He received a call from an acquaintance, listening to the dude talk about the streets while he waited for Maxine. Finally, he told the man he'd speak to him later and hung up, rubbing his hands together in anticipation.

Maxine turned up, and the pair had drinks, relaxing on the sofa. Cameron grinned, giving her a once over as she sipped her liquor. She was curly-haired and round-cheeked, with glittering dark eyes and a nice smile. They went way back, but they had never been able to make it work. Not that Cameron had really tried.

'Why did you fall out with your man?' He asked. Maxine shot him a calculating look.

'Do you really care?'

Cameron shook his head.

'I don't mind you telling me, though.'

'There's no real reason. It's like he just stopped trying. He's more interested in looking at women on his *Explore* page than spending time with me. I told him I needed a break to see how he would react, and it was like he didn't even care.'

Cameron rolled his eyes. Women annoyed him. He wasn't one for playing games, and part of him was proud that Maxine's boyfriend hadn't fallen for her ploy.

'Maybe you're just not a fun person,' he said. Maxine glared at him.

'Just because I don't want to sit around and play computer games, doesn't mean I'm not fun.'

Cameron grinned, finishing his drink and moving closer.

'That's fine with me. I'm not interested in playing computer games right now either . . .'

He kissed her, and Maxine didn't resist. After a moment, the kiss intensified, the pair pulling their bodies closer together. There was an urgency between them, a desire for an immediate release. Cameron pulled off his bottoms and adjusted Maxine's position on the sofa. She eyed him hungrily as he hovered above her, making her wait a beat before giving her what she wanted.

You're not the only one who can play games, he thought, as he took her there and then.

After, they rested, smoked and drank some more, then went at it again. It wasn't the same the second time around. The hunger and desire had gone, but Maxine was there and available, which was enough.

Cameron lounged on the sofa, sipping another drink and watching Maxine get dressed. He liked the fact she hadn't tried staying the night. Making women breakfast in the morning wasn't one of his favourite things to do.

'You heard about that event in town at the weekend? That London guy is meant to be DJing. I can't remember his name.'

Cameron nodded.

'Yeah, me and my people are gonna pass through. You going?'

'I was thinking about it,' admitted Maxine. 'If I see you there, you're buying me a drink.'

'Count on it,' said Cameron. 'Your Uber is here.'

Cameron locked the door behind Maxine, happy that he'd called her around. There were no strings, and he hadn't had to listen to her prattle on about her feelings too much. He wondered how long it would take before she ended up back with her partner. It was clear what she would do for attention, and Cam questioned her motives.

Maybe she just wanted some freedom. Some time to explore and have fun. It reinforced his misgivings when it came to women. It was ironic that the only girl he had been with that he thought wouldn't have cheated on him was his friend's girlfriend.

Anika was besotted with Cameron in their short time together. She worshipped him, which was fine at first, but he quickly became annoyed with it. He considered for a moment whether she would do to Spence what Maxine had her boyfriend. Cameron suspected she would. Maybe not in all circumstances, but almost definitely in some.

It would be easy for her to get away with it, he mused. Spence was a hard worker, and was often out for long stretches. Still, he realised, he had no reason to care. Spence was in love with her, and they were together.

Pushing the thoughts aside, he yawned and went upstairs. He'd mention the event to Natty tomorrow, and make sure they were still on.

CHAPTER EIGHT

BY THE FOLLOWING DAY, Cameron had woken up in a better mood, with his mind clearer. Having briefly considered the possibility of consulting his friends for money advice, his resolve had strengthened.

It took more than brains to make it in the streets, Cameron thought as he considered Spence's demeanour. Now more than ever, courage, resilience and ruthlessness were coveted. He was sure he would become a success. It was just a matter of time.

As he finished his breakfast and sipped his coffee, he considered which category Natty would fall into. The fact that he struggled to place him was troubling. Pushing the thoughts away, he wiped his mouth, stood up and placed his plate and cup in the sink.

Later on, Cameron met with Natty and Spence. The pair came to Cameron's house, and they ate food and watched football. Cameron was enjoying the vibe, mentioning their planned night out, but Spence just wanted to talk business, which annoyed him.

They were friends. They had plenty of time to talk about

Elijah and the streets, but just talking about business made it seem like they weren't as close as Cameron thought.

It didn't help that Natty was in a bad mood and barely responded to the pair. Spence managed to get him to talk about his issues, and Cameron resisted the urge to shake his head when Natty admitted that he and Lorraine had argued.

Cameron couldn't believe it. He didn't know what was wrong with his friends, but when he heard Spence trying to give Natty advice, he couldn't hold back any longer.

'Fucking hell, Spence. Are you still trying to pretend Anika hasn't changed you? You never used to talk all this nonsense before.'

Spence glared at him. Cameron was surprised at the fire in his eyes.

'It's okay to have different opinions, Cam. We don't always have to agree on everything. You think I talk to her about street shit? *Our shit?*'

'Anika got in your head with some nonsense, and now you're trying to do the same with Natty,' he sneered. He couldn't believe Spence was trying to get tough with him.

'You need to grow up,' Spence snapped. 'Anika hasn't changed me, but if women *do* have that effect, you should try harder to get one.'

Cameron's mouth formed a hard line, not liking Spence's words. He wasn't Spence. He wasn't soft, and he certainly didn't need a girlfriend.

'Make sure you ask for permission tomorrow. Wouldn't want her to cry if you go out otherwise.'

'For fucks sake, Cam—'

'Enough!' Natty roared, startling Cameron. 'Both of you shut the fuck up, because you're getting on my nerves. I don't know what is going on with you two, but you need to fix it, because this back-and-forth crap is annoying.'

Finishing his drink, Natty shot to his feet and stormed out.

Silence ensued, and Cameron glanced at Spence, the argument all but forgotten.

'He's too emotional,' Cameron mumbled. Spence sighed and shook his head. He left a short while later, and Cameron stared at the television, thinking about the way Natty had gone off. He knew Natty had a temper, but as far as he was concerned, he was choosing this stress. He didn't need to be in this situation. Lorraine wasn't his girlfriend, and her kid wasn't Natty's. The fact he was directing his temper at his friends didn't sit well with Cameron.

They seemed to be changing more every day. There was a vulnerability in Natty that he hadn't seen previously, which Cameron believed made him weaker.

He considered what this meant for him and the crew. If Natty and Spence continued down their current path, he would have to step up and fix them. It would take a lot of his effort, but he had no option.

Cameron was suddenly thankful for his plans over the weekend. It was a chance to kick back, blow off some steam and, possibly, get laid. It was exactly what he needed.

CHAPTER NINE

THE EVENT CAMERON had hyped and heard so much about, turned out to be a dud. The London DJ couldn't make it, and the replacement drafted in at the last minute played a terrible set.

Luckily, Natty was in a better mood — or seemed to be — and charmed a pretty Asian woman, who mentioned a party at an apartment in the city centre. They decided to attend, and Cameron was pleased they had. The women were better than he'd seen in the club, and there were plenty of them, along with decent liquor and drugs to indulge in.

Cameron recognised the host, a good-time girl called Ellie, whose rich dad funded her whole lifestyle. Apart from a hello, he kept it moving, not having much of a relationship with her.

Cameron and Spence were on speaking terms, but he was still annoyed by what he perceived as disrespect by his friend. They'd had a disagreement earlier in the day after Cameron made a comment about Anika. Spence had snapped, launching himself at Cameron. Fortunately, Natty was on hand to break things up.

Natty had turned from peace-maker to rival when they

arrived at the party. Despite Cameron seeing the pretty Asian girl first, Natty had swooped in and started sweet-talking her. It was typical of Natty when it came to women, and it was hard for Cameron not to be annoyed by it.

Wandering around the edges of the party now, Cameron's eyes widened when he saw Lorraine near the kitchen. He hadn't expected to see her, and wondered if Natty knew she was there. He doubted it. If he had, he'd be crowding her, or fawning over her like he usually did. A smile appeared on his face as he looked around to see if Natty was watching, before approaching. Lorraine smiled when she saw him.

'Hey, Cam.'

'Easy, Lorraine. Look at you. You look good.' Cameron's eyes roved over her body, liking her tight blue dress. He went in for a hug and squeezed her tightly, feeling her stiffen before letting her go.

'Thanks. You too,' she said, looking past him. 'Is Nat with you?'

Cameron inwardly seethed. It was always the same thing. She wasn't interested in talking to him. All she cared about was Natty. *When it suited her.* When it didn't, she was tapping up his opps.

'He's around somewhere,' Cameron dismissively said, keeping his annoyance off his face. 'You know how Natty gets down. He's probably getting some numbers or sliding off with someone.' Lorraine's face fell, and Cameron revelled in it. 'Seriously, though . . . you look sexy. I haven't seen you look so good before.' Cameron locked eyes with Lorraine, letting her know his intentions, having broken her down by mentioning Natty and other women.

To his chagrin, Lorraine stepped back, again looking past him.

'Thanks. Have a good time, Cam.' Lorraine walked off. Cameron glared after her, feeling slighted by the disrespect. Obviously, Lorraine was trying to get to Natty because she saw him as the leader of their little crew. Everyone did. He was sick of it. The desire to step up burned within Cameron. He needed something to happen. He couldn't stay at this level all of his life.

After a while, Cameron ended up with Spence and Natty. He watched Natty approach Lorraine, and to his secret glee, it didn't turn out well. Despite looking out for him earlier, Lorraine seemed angry with Natty now, and Cameron was glad, hoping what he'd said about Natty had caused the argument.

———

As the night went on, the party grew more unglued. Before long, Cameron was watching Natty angrily get into it with Wonder, who he knew was a member of Elijah's crew. Happy to be delving further into drama, Cameron had Natty's back, ignoring Spence's attempts to calm down the situation. He wanted Natty angry. He wanted them to set it off, with people around. He wanted the clout that would come from the encounter. The old Natty was back, and Cameron was ready for it.

Until Lorraine interfered. She took Natty away, and the moment settled, with Wonder and his boys retreating. Cameron and Spence shared a look.

'That was close,' said Spence.

'We should have fucked them up,' said Cameron, muscles tensing.

'No good would come of it,' said Spence. 'All it would have done is cause further problems.'

'Sometimes that needs to happen, bro,' said Cameron, staring at his friend. He needed him to understand. 'We're in the jungle. The streets aren't easy, and people thinking you can be disrespected, in private or in public, is not on.'

'It's deeper than that,' replied Spence. 'There's a right way to do things, and that way is more profitable than getting into a mess over nothing.' Spence sighed. 'I'm gonna get off, anyway. If anything happens, ring me, but I think the drama is over for now.'

Sourly, Cameron touched fists with his friend, knowing Spence was right. People had returned to normal, the earlier drama forgotten. Soon, Natty made his way back inside, accompanied by Elijah, to Cameron's surprise. Evidently, the pair had shared words, because soon Wonder came over to apologise to Natty.

The party continued, and Cameron watched Natty get drunker. When Ellie approached, Cameron wondered if she would throw Natty out. She stood in front of them, her right hand on her hip, eyes narrowed. She was a curvy brunette with deep blue eyes, a smattering of freckles across her nose, fake eyelashes and white nails.

'Do you want a drink?' Natty asked, which Cameron thought was brave of him.

Ellie shook her head.

'I should kick you out after all the trouble you caused,' she replied.

Natty grinned, which only made Ellie's scowl deepen. Taking her hand, he stroked her fingers. Cameron shook his head. *Only Natty . . .*

'I'm sorry, Ellie. I didn't mean to start a madness in the middle of your party.'

Ellie's face reddened as she tried to compose herself, flustered at the sudden closeness.

'You should be sorry,' she replied.

'Good thing I am then. There'll be nothing but good vibes the rest of the night. I promise.'

Shaking her head dazedly, Ellie wandered off.

'Ellie's into you, bro,' Cameron said after a few moments. Natty shrugged, not reacting. 'Sorry, I forgot; you're only bothered about sexy Lorraine,' Cameron went on, realising he wasn't going to get a response.

'Lorraine can fuck off.' Natty scowled.

'That's what you say. Prove it,' Cameron said.

'How?'

'Go for Ellie.'

To Cameron's shock and growing glee, Natty did precisely that. Soon, the pair were kissing as people cheered them on, then they stumbled to Ellie's bedroom. Cameron followed, taking out his phone and recording them kissing for a few moments, until clothing started being removed.

He didn't know why he'd done it, but figured he and Natty could laugh about it later. He also liked the leverage it would provide. Natty was becoming more and more difficult to entice out in recent times. Perhaps the video would prove useful in the future.

CHAPTER TEN

THE NEXT DAY, Cameron's bad mood returned. Natty had come over, back to his regular self, and had given him a lecture about Spence. Cameron didn't like being talked down to, and loathed that Natty was taking sides against him.

Cameron wasn't sure how to handle it. Despite his recent misgivings about his friends, Natty had more power than he did. He was the de-facto leader of their clique, and that wasn't going to change. Spence's surge in influence bothered Cameron more than anything. Their order had been well-established; Spence and Cameron operating on the same level, with the same responsibilities. Spence was developing and catching the eyes of the right people, which Cameron didn't find fair. His friends' family connections to the streets seemed to be putting him at an unfair disadvantage.

Cameron's phone rang later, long after Natty had gone. He didn't recognise the number, but answered anyway.

'Yeah?'

'Cameron? It's Marlon.'

'Easy. What's up?' Cameron replied, buoyed that Marlon had called him.

'I need something handling, and I think you're the man to

do it,' said Marlon, sounding agitated. Cameron wondered what it was. Not that it mattered. He was ready.

'What do you need?'

'Not over the phone. I'm gonna text you an address, and I want you to come and see me. Cool?'

'Cool. I'll be there ASAP.' Cameron hung up. When the address came through moments later, he grinned. Things were about to change for the better, he was sure of it.

———

RUDY SIPPED A DRINK, in his usual spot at Delores's. It was his favourite spot to hang out, even when he wasn't handling business.

Delores was a good woman. Her husband had looked out for Rudy when he was younger, and he never forgot it. When the man died, and Delores's son got himself locked up, Rudy began stopping in on her, ensuring she was okay and that she had what she needed. Eventually, this led to him using her home as an office, and ensuring she was adequately compensated.

Rudy was thinking about Nathaniel, sure he could be the lynchpin in the new world Rudy wanted to build. He had all the tools; he was strong, decisive, respected and skilled in whatever role he was put into. There was just his temperament to deal with — his immaturity.

It was mid-afternoon, and Rudy had already fielded numerous phone calls about Nathaniel nearly fighting with Elijah's men. He wasn't sure how he would handle it, or how he could make Nathaniel understand how ignorant his actions were, but he would do so.

Later, Elijah came to see him.

'Hello, Delores,' he said, as Rudy led him to the kitchen where the woman was seasoning food. In response, she gave him a look, sniffed, then went back to what she was doing.

Elijah's eyes narrowed, but Rudy chuckled, amused by the scene. Elijah was one of those strange people who needed everyone to like him, and Rudy was sure it irked him that Delores never had any time for him.

'Give us a few minutes, please, Delores,' Rudy said. Delores washed her hands, covered the food, and left the kitchen. Elijah shook his head.

'That is one cold woman,' he commented.

'Don't worry about that. Tell me about the party.'

'Figured you'd have heard about that,' said Elijah. 'There's not much to tell. Your boy got into it with Wonder and a few others. They were arguing about a woman, and Natty grabbed a bottle. Apparently, he was ready to smash it over Wonder's head. They rang me, and I came and talked to him. I think he was ready to fight me too, before we spoke.'

'Okay,' said Rudy. Elijah's story matched the others he had heard.

'He won't learn, Rudy. You know that. I've worked with people like him. They never do.' Elijah paused, looking at Rudy. When he didn't respond, he continued. 'If your plan doesn't work and he becomes a problem, I hope you have a contingency plan in place. If you need to use one of my men, Raider would happily—'

'No!' The anger in Rudy's voice surprised even him. Elijah's eyes widened, slighted by the interruption.

'Why not?'

Rudy's eyes narrowed. 'You're sharp, Elijah. It's the main reason we work together. Do I really need to explain why Mitch Dunn's nephew being killed might be a bad thing?'

Elijah grunted, but didn't respond.

'Maybe I do. If Nathaniel is killed, we won't be able to move in Leeds. Everyone will be a suspect, and that will do nothing but hold us back.' He fingered the glass on the table before him, then met Elijah's eyes again. 'I'll speak with Nathaniel. In the meantime, stick to the plan.'

RICKY BLACK

CAMERON MET Marlon at a house just off Shepherds Lane. When he walked in and saw the furious look on Marlon's face, he immediately thought he had done something wrong.

'Everything good?' He asked, watching Marlon pace the room, fury etched on his face. Maybe it had been stupid to turn up without letting anyone know where he was. He wasn't scared of Marlon personally, but he was close to Rudy, and had more clout than Cameron did.

'No. Everything is not good,' Marlon snapped, Cameron's brain scrambling to think what he might have done. Marlon took a deep breath, visibly calming down.

'I've got a little brother; Ron. He goes to college in town, and he's a good kid. Works hard, stays off the roads, and doesn't cause problems.' Marlon's jaw tensed. 'This fucker from Morley is troubling him. I don't know why, and I don't care. If you handle it for me, it won't be forgotten.'

Cameron needed little time to think about it. This was the opportunity he had been waiting for. He didn't care what the issue was, or why it had transpired. All he cared about was that he could finally step up if he sorted this. The unspoken rewards he would receive, were clear to him.

'Gimme a name and where I can find him, and I'll sort it. Your brother won't have any more problems with him,' Cameron promised.

IT DIDN'T long to track down the guy who had been making Ron's life hell. Cameron found him in a pub, half-drunk, laughing with a group of people. The man wasn't small. He had some muscle to him, and was hard-eyed, and Cameron could see how he might be a problem, especially to a good kid more focused on studying than fighting.

Cameron had kept his distance as the man left the pub, checking no one was watching, and that his hood was still up. As the man turned the corner after leaving the pub, Cameron struck, hitting the man in the back with a small led pipe he'd hidden in the folds of his hoody. The man went down with a scream, but Cameron didn't let up, hitting him twice more, then repeatedly kicking him in the head and stomach.

'You need to watch who you're trying to bully,' he snarled, before bringing down the pipe on the man's arm, hearing the sickening crack and subsequent screams. After a final kick to the head, he hurried away, breathing hard, adrenaline coursing through his veins as he grinned.

A short while later, he was back with Marlon, grinning over the beating he'd given the bully. Marlon had his phone in his hand, and hadn't acknowledged Cameron yet.

'You handled it then?' He finally said.

'He won't be troubling anyone for a while. I definitely broke a couple of bones,' said Cameron, raising his chin, ready for the adulation. This was it. This was the moment he stepped up.

'Good. Thanks for handling that.'

The air shifted within Cameron, and he rapidly deflated, coming down from his high.

That was it? That was all he got for risking his freedom?

'It's . . . cool,' Cameron finally said. Marlon glanced at him, then returned to his phone.

'That's all, bro. Thanks again for sorting it.'

Cameron's feet led him away from the house on autopilot. He had been so sure that he was about to get a promotion at the very least, but he'd got nothing, just an offhand thank you. He drove away in a funk, one indisputable truth rattling around his brain.

Marlon had hustled him. He had manipulated him into handling a problem with no promise of a reward. In his haste, Cameron had jumped at the chance. Just like he had with the *investment opportunity.* He could feel the rage building within him.

Was being tough enough anymore? It didn't feel it. Spence wasn't finding himself in these situations; being hustled by people who Cameron believed couldn't stand toe-to-toe with him.

He clenched his hands, balling them into fists. Taking a deep breath, he focused on the road and tried to quell his growing frustrations.

CHAPTER ELEVEN

RUDY WASN'T in a good mood. He'd told Elijah he would deal with Nathaniel, but had yet to speak to him.

He wasn't sure what he would do with the wayward man-child. He truly believed Nathaniel was the future of the organisation. Under his tutelage, Nathaniel would rise far. If he learned to listen and properly conduct himself.

For Rudy, responsibility was a cornerstone of doing business. Whether that be making responsible decisions that positively impacted the crew, or taking responsibility when your actions brought heat to the organisation.

Avoiding taking responsibility was something Rudy wouldn't tolerate. Having attempted to call and text Nathaniel multiple times without success, Rudy had resorted to scouring the streets in an attempt to find him.

After a while, he did just that, ordering his driver to bring the car to a stop beside Nathaniel, who stood, laughing and smoking weed with his friends on the street. They froze when they saw Rudy, but he kept his eyes firmly on Nathaniel, who looked like a kid that had been caught red-handed.

'Seventeen phone calls. Eight text messages. No response,'

said Rudy. Nathaniel met his gaze. As the moment stretched with neither man speaking, Nathaniel finally rubbed his forehead.

'I've been busy. I was gonna get back to you today.'

'Not too busy to be sitting outside, getting high and joking around, when you could be working, though?' Rudy shook his head. He didn't want to waste words on him in front of his friends. 'Get in the car.'

Nathaniel's eyes narrowed. Rudy hoped he didn't start acting the fool, but would handle it if he did.

'You don't need to come at me like that, Rudy,' he snarled. With a huff, he took a hit of the joint, then slapped hands with Cameron and Spence. As Nathaniel climbed into the car, his friend Cameron began laughing. He shot his friend a hard look, and Cameron's laughter evaporated. Rudy approved of the action.

The car pulled away, no one speaking. Rudy kept his eyes ahead, ignoring Nathaniel's fidgeting.

'Where are we going?' He finally asked.

'Figured we'd go to the pub, seeing as you're so fond of drinking recently,' said Rudy.

'I barely drink,' Nathaniel petulantly responded. Rudy ignored him. Eventually, they pulled up outside a pub in Middleton.

Rudy led the way. The pub was one of his favourite spots to hang out. It had an old-fashioned layout, with an old wooden partition and several tables, chairs and stools that had seen better days. The burgundy decor was clean, but the stench of beer hung heavily in the air. Rudy nodded to a fleshy, grey-haired landlady, and after a minute, they had a table. A football match played in the background, capturing the bar's attention.

The landlady took their orders. Rudy ordered a coke, and Nathaniel reluctantly ordered a lemonade. Nathaniel glanced around the pub, before finally sighing, focusing on Rudy.

'Talk me through it,' said Rudy, sipping his coke.

Nathaniel didn't immediately speak. Yells of encouragement from the punters distracted him for a few seconds.

'What do we need to talk through?' He finally replied.

Rudy's nostrils flared. Putting his glass down, he rubbed his temples. Nathaniel was off to a bad start, and Rudy was debating whether a punishment would fix him. Evidently, he noticed Rudy's anger, because he spoke again.

'Wonder ran his mouth.'

'So?'

Nathaniel shrugged. Rudy shook his head.

'What am I supposed to do with you . . .?'

'You tell me. I don't get any real sense of direction nowadays,' Nathaniel flippantly replied. Rudy's eyes widened, shocked at Nathaniel's audacity. He couldn't believe he'd said that. Despite his age and demeanour, Rudy's fists clenched and unclenched. He didn't know where the disrespect was coming from, but he wouldn't stand for it, no matter what Nathaniel's surname was.

'If you're ever going to make anything of yourself, you need to start working out when it's the time to close your mouth and do what's best for the people above you.'

'Wonder ran his mouth. Not me.'

'Nathaniel, we're trying to do business here. Make money. Is this the time for your little gangster shit?'

'There's no gangster shit here.'

'You're just fighting over a girl you're not even involved with. Where's the sense in that?'

Rudy couldn't fathom it. Nathaniel had always been free and loose where women were concerned, and had slept with a significant amount, in and around Chapeltown. Rudy didn't understand how he had managed to get entangled with a woman who already had a child, along with other baggage.

Nathaniel's jaw tightened.

'I wasn't fighting over her. It's not about her. It's about them.'

'Elijah's people are harmless, so I need you to ignore them and stop making the wrong moves.'

Nathaniel sipped his drink, eyes blazing. Rudy sighed, sensing the younger man growing angrier.

'Nathaniel, the streets are always watching. I don't need to tell you that. Your Unc is watching too, and this dumb shit always gets back to him. I know you're unhappy with how things are, but you need to see this as an opportunity to prove yourself.'

Nathaniel shot him another look.

'What more can I do?'

Rudy nearly laughed.

'What is it you think you *have* done? You have a problem with authority, Nathaniel, and you're too quick to flip out at the wrong times.'

Nathaniel's eyes narrowed, but he didn't have an answer. Realising an answer wasn't coming, Rudy continued.

'You have everything you need to get to the top. To lead. Lose that chip off your shoulder and go after what you want, but do it for you, not for what you think people want you to do.'

Nathaniel shook his head. 'I don't care what people think of me.'

'Yes, you do. People know it, and if you let them, they will use it,' said Rudy firmly. Nathaniel scowled as the crowd noise increased again.

'You could have spoken to my uncle at any time and told him to elevate me, but you haven't. Save the preaching.'

Rudy's eyes bore into Nathaniel's younger pair. Even now, after all the advice Rudy had shared, he was still being obstinate. Refusing to listen. Defiantly pressing ahead with his nonsense. Rudy had seen this before from a headstrong man with the *Dunn* surname.

'First, watch your mouth. Second, I don't tell your Unc anything. Outside of your mum, nobody does.' Rudy's nostrils flared. 'You've been in the game long enough to understand that one wrong move can have disastrous effects. It can even cost you your life.'

'If Raider even looks at me wrong, I'll finish him.'

Rudy again shook his head.

'Is that all you are?' He asked, voice almost a whisper. 'You wanna be like your old man, is that it?'

'Don't talk about my dad.' Nathaniel's fists clenched. Rudy didn't care. Nathaniel needed to understand. Years ago, his dad had foolishly wanted to lead a campaign to wipe out other rival dealers, determined to put their crew at the top. He'd refused to listen to solid advice, pushing away everyone that wanted to help him.

'I knew him, remember? Roughest of the rough, putting bodies in the ground. Where did it get him? It got him de—'

'I said, don't talk about my fucking dad.' Nathaniel leapt to his feet, their drinks clattering to the floor. 'He was more of a man than you could ever be. Keep his damn name out of your mouth.'

Before Rudy could reply, Nathaniel stomped from the pub, leaving a shocked, silent crowd in his wake.

RUDY LEFT THE PUB, having watched Nathaniel storm off. He needed to consider whether banking on him was the right move.

Now, more than ever, Nathaniel needed to keep his wits about him. People, Elijah included, wanted to see him fail.

Rudy reached Tia Dunn's home, telling the driver he would call later if he needed him. When he entered, Tia was reading a book, which she put aside when she saw him, sliding to her feet and smiling as they shared a kiss. Even after so many years, she still did something to Rudy that no other woman did. Tia was barely over five and a half feet tall, and had light brown eyes and delicate facial features. Rudy was enamoured with her full lips. She didn't smile much, but it made the moments where she did mean more.

'I wasn't sure I would see you tonight,' she said.

'My meeting finished earlier than I expected, and I needed some time away from everything,' Rudy admitted, finally relaxing after the tense meeting.

'Are you hungry?' Tia asked.

'Ravenous,' Rudy replied, a playful smile on his face.

'You sit down. I'll warm some food up.'

Rudy complied, slumping down into the seat and grabbing the TV remote.

Later, Rudy put his plate to one side, rubbing his stomach. In the kitchen, Tia was second only to Delores. He had known her a long time, and had worked with her ex-husband, Tyrone Dunn.

As the years passed, Tia had retained her looks, but she'd slowed down in general, and was happy not doing much. That being said, Rudy always took her seriously. She was a sharp woman, who could tear people apart with words if they weren't prepared.

'Were you meeting with my son?' She asked, as the pair sipped drinks on the sofa. Rudy glanced at the television, wondering who had won the football match that had been playing in the pub.

'We had words, but they didn't go well.'

'Why not?' Tia leaned forward. Rudy told her the story, starting with Nathaniel getting into trouble at the party, then their subsequent meeting.

'He's his father's son,' said Tia, her face devoid of emotion. 'He's all Ty.'

'Things might have to change in the future if Nathaniel can't play along,' said Rudy, hiding his annoyance at Tia's words. Tyrone Dunn had been Rudy's best friend, and he knew the man better than anyone, but he didn't like the idea of Nathaniel being like his dad. He was fond of the young man, and cared for him in his own way, wanting him to conduct himself properly, and to take on better habits.

'Ty has been dead a long time. As we both know, he died for a reason . . . he couldn't see the forest for the trees,' said Rudy, pushing away the guilt he felt over that act. 'The crew wouldn't have ascended as it did if Ty had remained involved. He wanted to ruin us.'

'I know this already, Rudy,' said Tia. Rudy shook his head. As cold as Tia could be, he still loved her. He hugged her closely, kissing the top of her head, enjoying the feel of her.

'Nathaniel might end up getting hurt,' he said, looking deeply into her eyes. Tia sighed, still meeting his gaze.

'Life is harsh sometimes. I trust you to do the right thing, Rudy.'

DAYS LATER, to Rudy's surprise, he heard from Elijah.

'What's up?' He asked, holding the phone to his ear and looking all around, despite the fact he was alone indoors. It was a tough habit to break.

'The meeting with your boy went well. He surprised me,' said Elijah, getting to the point.

'Surprised you how?'

'I always thought he was just a brute, but he's sharper than I thought. Tenacious too.'

'I told you. This is why I wanted Nathaniel involved with us. Little London will be the perfect training ground for him.'

'60/40 split, though . . . why am I the one getting short-changed in this?'

Rudy shook his head at Elijah's short-sightedness.

'You should have negotiated better if you had a problem

with it. It doesn't matter, anyway. You'll make it back in the long run and then some.'

Elijah didn't say anything, but Rudy knew his words had hit home.

'I'll speak with Nathaniel later and make sure he understands his task.'

CHAPTER TWELVE

CAMERON LEANED back on his sofa, watching Spence and Natty. They had been in his house a short while, but something seemed different. He couldn't put his finger on it, but the energy in the room was strange. He assumed it was because of his back and forth with Spence, but couldn't be sure.

Natty had brought food for everyone, and they made small talk as they ate. When they were finished, Natty took the lead.

'The meeting went well. We're in business,' he said.

Cameron grinned, glancing at Spence and noting his reaction was the same.

'How was Elijah?' Spence asked.

'He was cool. We had a decent chat,' said Natty.

'Do you trust him?' Spence had his eyes on Natty.

'I do.'

Cameron snorted. Natty had hated Elijah and his crew for the longest time, but now his opinion had changed . . . just like that.

'Couple' meetings and you're sold on the guy,' he said.

'I'm willing to give him the benefit of the doubt,' replied Natty.

'It's in his best interests to play it safe. If not, it's war. I don't think any of us want that,' said Spence.

Cameron was conflicted. On one hand, he hoped it would lead to more opportunity and increased pay. It was sorely needed, he thought, as he wiped the face of his fake watch with his thumb.

On the other hand, Cameron's frustrations were at boiling point. He needed an outlet, and he wondered whether a war would provide that for him. A place to release his frustrations and anger, improving his street reputation in the process. In body or in spirit, those who made their mark in war were eternalised in Chapeltown.

The last true street war in 2015 was testament to this, and the streets still spoke fondly of the people involved. Cameron needed that clout. He needed to be respected and talked about with reverence. His challenge was making that happen.

'I don't give a fuck about war. I stay ready,' Cameron said, puffing out his chest.

'The last *war* was between Roc and D-Mo.' Natty responded, his eyebrow arched.

Cameron shook his head. To him, Roc and D-Mo were a joke. Internet beef that ended with both losing their livelihood. He was thinking bigger.

'I'm talking about Teflon's wars. Those guys are legends.'

'The game is bigger than that, Cam. I want a career and the money that goes with it. I don't want pointless clout,' said Natty.

Cameron shook his head. Natty was talking nonsense.

'Behave, Nat. As long as I've known you, you've wanted a name on the streets. Look at the shit you used to get into, trying to build a rep.' He sneered. Cameron couldn't take it. The more time Natty spent with Spence, the softer he seemed to become. Cameron believed he was rubbing off on Natty in all the wrong ways.

'It's okay to change. I still think Elijah is sneaky, but the plan is a good one and makes a lot of sense. We can do our legwork and drive around the area, check things out.'

Cameron's nose wrinkled. He had no intention of going to Little London.

'It's a shithole. There's no point.'

Natty glanced at Spence, who didn't say anything. Again, Cameron's eyes watched the pair. *They were up to something.*

'With all the extra work I'm gonna be doing to get this off the ground, someone needs to step up and run the crew day-to-day,' Natty started. Cameron straightened in anticipation, his eyes widening.

This was his moment, and he was ready.

'Spence, you're up.'

Cameron froze, watching as Spence nodded, giving Natty a small smile. A roaring anger took over him. He wanted to tear his friends to shreds for the disrespect.

Spence over him? What the hell was Natty thinking?

'Are you serious? Did you forget I've been down since day one and always had your back?' He snarled. He could feel his anger, and could only imagine what it looked like to his friends.

'Course not. You've never shown any interest in running things. I don't see what the big deal is,' Natty replied.

'Spence hasn't either,' Cameron pointed out, but Natty shook his head.

'Not true. We've had conversations in the time about how things run, and what to look out for. He's contributed strong ideas.'

'Why haven't you had the same conversations with me?' Cameron demanded.

'Because you never asked, and Spence sought me out to learn. That's the difference.'

Cameron frowned, scowling at Natty.

'Well, I want the information too.'

'Good. You can learn it from Spence.' Natty stared into his eyes. 'This is a big move for all of us. We can use it to really put ourselves on the map.'

Cameron's scowl didn't shift. His anger hadn't abated. They had played him for a fool. Spence running the team over him was ludicrous.

'It's a big move for you lot more than me. I've been repping this crew since day one, putting myself on the line when we needed it, and I'm being left behind,' he snarled.

'Cam, it's not like that,' added Spence, but Cameron shook his head. He didn't need Spence getting involved.

'Yeah, it is like that. You didn't speak to me about any of this. You just expected me to fall in line. That's fucked up.' Cameron jerked his hand at Spence. 'How can you depend on this guy to lead? He can't even drag himself away from his girl.'

'Are we going on about that again?' retorted Spence. Cameron shot him a scornful look, shaking his head. He was so close to telling him some home truths. He could ruin Spence if he wanted to, and that power excited him.

'You need some time to chill and get your head around things,' said Natty. Cameron responded by lighting a spliff and flicking on the television. He was done talking to them. Natty held up his hand.

'This is exactly why you're not ready to lead, bro,' he said. 'You lose your temper, and then nothing else matters. You just switch off.'

Cameron took a long drag of the spliff, shrugged, then continued watching the television.

CAMERON SAID nothing when his friends left. He'd had enough of the pair. They were supposed to be a team, yet he had to suffer rampant disrespect, time and time again.

How long was he supposed to put up with it?
When would he catch a break?

The pair had manipulated him. They were a team, yet they were willing to move on without him. He doubted his name had ever been in contention. It was all a twisted game, and he was sick of it.

Now more than ever, he needed to get ahead, but his options were limited. He could no longer count on his friends. He would need to find another way of making his name and fortune.

Cameron smoked another spliff, still fuming over the situation. He didn't know how he would handle the gall of taking orders from Spence, sure his friend would lord it over him.

When his phone rang, he was two drinks and a spliff deep, debating ignoring the call. When he saw the number, his eyes widened, and he grabbed the phone.

'Yeah?'

'Cam, I've got another job for you, if you're interested.'

Cameron weighed it up for a moment. Marlon had played him for a fool last time, and it was possible he would again.

Ultimately, he didn't have a choice. His friends had forsaken him. Marlon was his best shot.

'I'm down, fam. What do you need.'

'You know Christian. The white boy?'

Cameron did. Christian was a known cokehead who he'd dealt with in the past.

'Yeah, I know him.'

'He's late paying back for some stuff he got from us on tick. Pick the money up, but send him a message too. It's not the first time, and we can't have him taking liberties.'

Cameron hadn't known Christian was getting drugs on credit. It surprised him; he'd always thought the man was rich enough to buy his drugs outright, but this clearly wasn't the case.

'I'll take care of it,' he said.

'That's my guy,' said Marlon. 'When you're done, I need you to go to a spot on Francis Street—'

'Delores's?' Cameron blurted out. He'd been there with Natty on multiple occasions.

There was a pause on the other end.

'You know it?' Marlon finally asked.

'Yeah.'

'Good. That makes things easier. Report there when you're done. Rudy wants a word.'

CHAPTER THIRTEEN

THE FOLLOWING MORNING, Cameron had a lot on his mind. He remained furious about being passed over, wondering more about the agendas of his friends. Natty could have given Cameron the rub, and Cameron could have worked with Spence to toughen up the crew and make them stronger.

Instead, he hadn't even been an afterthought. Natty had picked Spence, and that was that.

Spence had won again, Cameron mused, drinking coffee. Or, at least, he thought he had, playing house with Anika, not knowing what she was really like.

Cameron's friends were forsaking him, but he was real to the core. If he couldn't elevate with his friends, he would branch out. Focusing on the job for Rudy was the best thing to do. If he handled it right, it could likely lead to more opportunities. It was time to think about himself at the expense of his team.

Cameron turned his thoughts to Christian. He didn't expect much, if any, resistance. Christian was soft, and a bit of a liability. People in the streets could be sneaky, though.

Cameron wondered if it was worth bringing backup, and for a fleeting second, he considered asking Natty.

After thinking it over for a few minutes, Cameron decided against it. Not only was he unsure about Natty's motives at present, he also didn't want to alert him to his moves unless necessary.

———

Cameron took a taxi down the street from Christian's address, then headed up the road, keeping his head down just in case anyone was watching.

He knocked at Christian's door, watching the man pale when he saw him. Christian was slightly taller than Cameron, with a ponytail and designer stubble, his t-shirt stretched tight around a gut accrued from excessive takeaways.

Cameron smiled.

'Hi mate. Are you going to invite me in?'

Christian glanced around the room, looking like he would rather be anywhere but there. Cameron chuckled.

'C'mon, bro. We're good, and I know you don't want to talk business on the doorstep where everyone can hear us.'

Christian's shoulders slumped, and he allowed Cameron to enter. They went to the living room. Cameron slumped into a seat on the sofa, then put his feet up on the coffee table. Christian's jaw tensed.

'Look, Cam. I'm sorry I've fallen behind. Some of the lads I work with have given me the runaround.'

'And that made you think you could give *us* the runaround too? You know that's not how the game works.'

'I know, but there was nothing I could do, and I didn't think you would be understanding if I approached you about it.'

'We'll never know, I guess.' Cameron shrugged. 'Do you have it now?'

Christian nodded. He left the room and returned with a plastic bag. Cameron looked inside at the contents, seeing the notes hastily banded together. He took them from the bag and began counting. His eyes narrowed as he neared the end of the count. Christian cleared his throat.

'Erm, look, I have most of it, but—'

'Why did you tell me you had it?'

'Because I didn't want you to think I was playing games.'

'You *are* playing games,' Cameron snapped. 'Rudy isn't a patient guy, and neither am I. First, you don't get in touch and keep ducking when we're trying to speak to you. Then, you say you've got the full eight grand, when you only have six. What the fuck is going on?'

'I'm sorry . . .'

'I don't wanna hear how sorry you are. Doesn't mean fuck all to me. Tell me what the hell is going on?' Cameron's feet slid from the table.

'I told you. I've got people slipping me, messing with my drugs, trying to put me out of business. Why do you think I'm so far behind?'

'I think you're a greedy little prick. You should have gotten in touch and didn't, so now we're gonna get deep.'

Christian stepped back as Cameron rose to his feet.

'C'mon, Cam, other than this, I've been loyal. You don't need to go on like that.'

Cameron sprang forward, covering the doorway so Christian couldn't escape. Christian put his hands up in surrender, but Cameron slammed his fist into his flabby stomach, then kicked him backwards, laughing when Christian toppled to the ground. He kicked him in the ribs when he tried to stand, then did the same thing again.

'You've been warned before about playing with us, you little prick.' Cameron kicked him after every word. 'You'll think twice about doing it again in future.'

Before he could hit Christian again, he heard a scream of

rage and turned. At the last second, he was able to get his hand up, instinctively deflecting the knife that hurtled towards his face. It cut deeply into his wrist, the snarling woman raising her hand to strike again.

'Bitch!' Cameron snarled, backhanding the woman and sending her flying across the room, the knife clattering to the ground. Groaning, she crawled towards it, slowly stretching out, feeling for the blade. As the tips of her fingers touched it, Cameron's boot came crashing down on her hand. Screaming in pain, she cradled her hand as Cameron moved closer, breathing hard.

'Shouldn't have involved yourself,' he said, drawing his foot back and kicking her in the ribs. She let out a groan of pain, holding her hand, rolling into the foetal position. He kicked her again.

'Stop it!' Christian yelled. 'I'm sorry, that shouldn't have happened. Please, just leave her alone.'

Cameron whirled toward Christian, his eyes blazing.

'I'm coming back tonight. You need to have the rest of the money, plus an extra five bills, or else.'

CAMERON TOUCHED HIS WRIST, still scowling. He'd not taken Christian seriously, and almost paid for it. He had been lucky to avoid the worst of the damage, but a shallow cut had been opened on his wrist, and in his rage, he'd reacted, feeling no remorse for either. He'd enjoyed having an outlet for his recent frustrations.

He took a deep breath, nervous about his meeting with Rudy. Despite begging Natty for an opportunity to speak with Rudy, he was anxious about dealing with him one-on-one, having always had the impression Rudy didn't like him. He wasn't sure how much this had to do with Natty's relationship with Rudy, but he didn't want it to negatively impact him.

Nodding to himself, he made his way toward Delores's place.

———

Rudy impassively watched Cameron approach, not expecting much from Nathaniel's wayward friend. Over the years, he'd received numerous negative reports about him. Cameron Greene had only got the job because of Nathaniel, and seemed to be a decent hustler, but he was a hothead, and Rudy didn't think that was the suitable type for Nathaniel to have around.

It was hard enough dealing with him as it was.

Rudy put the paperback he'd been reading to one side, as Cameron handed him the money he'd taken from Christian. Rudy began counting the money.

'You take a piece?' He asked. Cameron shook his head.

'Nah, I'd never do that. He gave me extra too, because of the runaround.'

Rudy smiled tightly. His eyes flicked to Cameron's injured hand.

'I figured you'd have kept the extra,' he admitted.

'It's not my money,' replied Cameron. Rudy surveyed him. Cameron had a stocky build, with surprisingly soft facial features. The eyes were hard, though, as Nathaniel's could be at times. He knew Cameron's background, including the fact he had grown up without a father. He wondered what effect that had on him.

Cameron not taking the extra money had surprised him. Based on what he knew about Cameron's profile, he figured he'd have done so.

'You're not that bad, are you . . . we definitely picked the right person for the job. You're loyal.' Rudy peeled off some notes. He held them out to Cameron. When Cameron reached, Rudy pulled back and added more to the pile.

Cameron thumbed through the money. His eyebrows rose.

'You didn't need to give so much. You said five.'

Rudy's eyebrows rose. He hadn't spoken with Cameron at all, never mind about the price, but figured it was something Marlon had agreed with him.

'Don't you want the extra?' He asked.

Cameron grinned. 'I didn't say that.'

'Good. Don't worry about it then. How did it go? Did Christian learn not to fuck around going forward?'

Cameron nodded. 'I gave him a beating he won't forget. His girl got involved, so I had to smack her around too.'

Rudy shrugged. He didn't care about Christian, and doubted he would learn his lesson. It was in the man's nature. He tried taking liberties after getting comfortable, took his warning, then eventually tried again. 'I'm sure she deserved it. How is Nathaniel doing?'

'Natty's the same as ever.'

'I know about the party in town you all went to a while back,' said Rudy. He'd noted Cameron almost rolling his eyes, inwardly amused by his restraint.

'What did you hear?'

'I heard he squared up to several of Elijah's men. You were there with him, right?'

'I was, so was Spence. That was Natty's thing, though. I backed my boy.'

'Like I said, you're loyal.' Rudy's eyes narrowed. He wanted to see how Cameron reacted, noting he'd instinctively straightened.

'Look, Natty is mad about a lot of things, but mostly that you've taken so long to give him more to do. He's here grinding, we all are, and we all want more.'

'Is that Nathaniel talking, or you?' Rudy hadn't expected such a reveal from so little probing. As much as he was re-evaluating his opinion of Cameron, this proved that he still had a lot to learn.

'Natty's the leader. I watch his back, same as always.'

'We have a lot riding on this, as you know. Nathaniel and I have cleared the air, and he's getting on board, but we both know how he can get. I need you to keep him safe.'

'Natty can look after himself,' said Cameron.

'He doesn't always think. The day we left you and Spence, he threatened me in the middle of a pub.'

'What?' Cameron's eyes widened.

'I pushed him too far. Mentioned his dad,' said Rudy.

Cameron nodded, but said nothing. Rudy knew he understood. Nathaniel worshipped the legend of his dad.

'That'll do it. Natty doesn't take that shit laying down.'

'Regardless, keep an eye on him. You know how we do it. This will benefit everyone, and in the long run, everyone will make more. You're a good kid. That Spence is too. He's a student of the game. I spent time with dudes like *Teflon* and learned how they think. The game is the game. The money . . . the money can be absolutely everything. If we do it right. Are you with me?'

Cameron nodded, but Rudy noted the tightening of his face when Spence was mentioned. This was something he could use.

'I'll keep you posted on Natty. Cheers for the bonus,' said Cameron, turning to leave.

'Sit down,' said Rudy.

Cameron looked over his shoulder, brow furrowed in confusion. After a moment, he turned around and made his way back to Rudy, shifting awkwardly when he sat down.

'Is something wrong?'

'I like the fact you extorted more money out of Christian, but double-check in future before you do it. If he was a more lucrative punter, I'd have an issue with it.'

'Sorry,' said Cameron. Rudy could see him fighting not to scowl, again impressed.

'Don't worry about it. I know a lot about Nathaniel, Cameron . . . as you can imagine. I knew his dad, and I've worked with his uncle for a long time. I don't know much about you, however.'

'What do you want to know?' Cameron rubbed his knuckles. Rudy waited a moment before replying.

'You're playing the game. What do you want from it? Do you want to work with Nathaniel all of your life, or do you have a plan?'

'I want to be the main guy,' said Cameron quickly. He paused, almost embarrassed by the outburst, but when Rudy didn't react, he visibly relaxed.

'Everyone has that dream. What separates you from them?'

'This is all I've got,' said Cameron. 'I don't have a famous dad, or a famous uncle. People see Natty before they see me. Sometimes, they even see Spence. I've got balls, though. I'm here with you now, and I can look you in your face and let you know that I will be the main guy. I've been scraping by for years, watching everyone else get rich. I want my shot. I *need* my shot,' he finished. After a moment, he sighed, seemingly overwhelmed by his own speech.

Rudy was impressed, not believing Cameron would speak from the heart. There was a deep-seated need to be better than his friends. He had ambition, and Rudy knew he could easily twist this to suit his own needs.

'In order to get what you want on the streets, what would you be willing to do.'

Cameron didn't hesitate.

'Anything.'

'That's good to hear. I think I may be able to use you. If you work with me, you'll go far, that I promise.'

'I appreciate it, Rudy. I appreciate the opportunity. I already got snaked, so this is all I've got.'

'What happened?'

Rudy listened as Cameron spoke about the fact Natty had suggested Spence for promotion over him. He'd already known about this. In fact, when he and Nathaniel had made up, he had agreed with Nathaniel's decision to use Spence.

'Nathaniel doesn't always make the best decisions,' Rudy said. 'I need you to keep an eye on him, and help keep him on the straight and narrow. Can you do that for me?'

Cameron nodded.

'Yeah.'

'Good. I'll be in touch. You can let yourself out,' said Rudy, watching Cameron leave. He would speak with Elijah first, but Cameron would be a perfect addition to their scheme.

CHAPTER FOURTEEN

FOR A WHILE AFTER, Cameron felt good about the situation, and the way his meeting with Rudy had gone. He had an in with Rudy that he was sure would continue to benefit him long into the future, and he knew how important it was to keep that going.

Marlon had spoken to him afterwards, having been briefed by Rudy on Cameron's involvement within the team. Another monetary bonus of one thousand pounds had been given to him, with no strings, and Marlon was even talking to him with some respect now, which was excellent.

Despite everything going well, Cameron still wanted revenge against Lodi. He'd heard nothing from the scammer since he had ripped him off, and no one in Chapeltown spoke about him. Philip had finished paying his debts, but Cameron decided to go and see him again, to see if he had heard anything about his wayward friend. His phone vibrated as he was leaving the house. His old friend — *Skinny Dave* — who had previously given him gambling tips, had another on a horse to win.

Cameron glanced at the message for a long moment, then went to his gambling app, putting fifty pounds on the horse.

With a terse *thank you* message to his contact, he stowed the phone and was on his way.

———

'Cam, you can't keep pulling up on me like this,' Philip moaned, when he opened the door to Cameron. He looked thinner than usual, and had dark circles under his eyes. Cameron wondered what was stressing him out, but didn't care enough to question him.

'Shut up, you little prick. You know why I'm here. Have you heard from your mate yet?'

Philip frantically shook his head. 'He's probably out of town, Cam. He'd be an idiot to stick around after ripping you off.'

'He's a fucking idiot in general for trying it, and you're just as bad for going along with it.'

'I told you already. I didn't—'

'Shut the fuck up!' Cameron backhanded Philip, sending him stumbling down the hallway. 'You know what you did. You introduced me to him, and it's your problem. You'd better recognise that shit is different now. I'm moving up in the world with the Dunns. Understand, I'm never gonna stop hunting this guy, which means I'm gonna be on your back too. Get it?'

Trembling, Philip nodded, touching his bloodied lip.

'Good. I'll be seeing you soon. You know what you need to do to stop all of this.'

Cameron left Philip, grinning, looking forward to the next time he made his life hell.

———

Later, Cameron was leaving the main spot, having completed a shorter shift. Things had gone by smoothly, to his chagrin. With Natty getting ready to make his move in the Little London area, Spence had already begun leading the crew. Cameron had hoped he would stumble, but so far, he was doing well, and people respected him.

Despite this, Cameron noted that some of the Dunn crew were generally looking at him differently, and treating him far more respectfully. He didn't know if this was down to Rudy and Marlon talking him up, but he liked it. It made him feel important.

Stifling a yawn, Cameron wondered if he could get Maxine to come over again. If she was back with her boyfriend, it would be tricky, but not impossible.

Anika flitted into his mind then, and he snorted, focusing on the road.

Just as Cameron reached home, Natty pulled up outside his house. He had Jaden with him, holding the young kid's hand as they approached.

'Yes, Cam,' Natty said. He touched Cameron's fist, then Jaden copied the action, which made Cameron smirk. Jaden was a decent kid, even if Natty had been a bit too quick to get involved in his life.

'What's up? Where are you lot coming from?' Cameron asked, ruffling Jaden's hair.

'We're just driving about. I was gonna take him to get some food,' said Natty.

'Where's his mum?'

'She's studying. I'm gonna bring her back something to eat too. I just wanted to stop by, make sure everything was okay,' said Natty. He pulled Jaden closer, and Cameron frowned when he saw the smile on the kid's face. He didn't know why it affected him so much, but Lorraine had her hooks into his friend.

Not only that, but when Cameron had spoken to her at Ellie's party, she'd dismissed him like he was nothing.

It was evident by the dynamic between Jaden and Natty

that they were close, and that galled him. Natty was being punked, and forced to raise Raider's kid. It wasn't right.

'You okay?' Natty asked, noting Cameron's change of mood. Cameron nodded, looking at Jaden.

'How's your dad, Jaden? Seen him lately?'

Jaden's face blanched, and Cameron almost felt sorry for him. He didn't know the last time Raider had bothered to see his son, but knew it was a touchy subject for all involved.

'What the hell?' Natty snapped, glaring at Cameron as Jaden visibly deflated.

'Sorry. It just came out,' said Cameron, knowing the damage was done. Natty and Jaden left shortly afterwards, and Cameron smiled to himself, hoping he'd thrown a spanner in the works.

Even if Natty didn't realise it, he was doing him a favour.

Later that night, Natty called him.

'Hey, fam. What's happening?' Cameron asked, but Natty wasn't in the mood.

'What the hell were you thinking, bringing up Raider like that in front of Jaden? You know what that situation's like.'

'Sorry, man. I didn't do it on purpose,' said Cameron. 'I thought maybe he'd been to see him lately. You brought him with you, and I was just making conversation. That's it.'

'Don't ever say anything like that around him again. Understand?'

Cameron's eyes narrowed as he gripped the phone tighter.

'Are you really coming at me like that, Nat?'

'He's a fucking child, Cam. If you wanna know if he's seen his dickhead dad, then ask me. Don't directly ask him and upset him.'

'I get it, man. I didn't think it was that deep,' said Cameron snidely. 'Just be careful, trying to play daddy to the kid. Lorraine might have an agenda, that's all.'

Natty paused for a moment before responding.

'You're the one that needs to be careful. Don't do that shit again.'

Natty hung up after that, leaving Cameron in shock. He knew how Natty could get, but he was surprised his friend had threatened him over Jaden. Cameron wondered if he had gone too far, but quickly dismissed it.

It wasn't his fault Natty was so sensitive nowadays.

———

Sometime later, Cameron found himself in a club near Call Lane, watching Anika. She'd been on his mind on and off, and he'd finally checked her social media, noting she would be out on this night for her friend Carmen's birthday. Cameron knew Carmen, but didn't like her, thinking she was dull and opinionated.

Lately, it was getting harder to shake the old thoughts about Anika. He found himself thinking back on their time together, wondering what she and Spence had that was so special.

Was it just the fact that Spence was more sensitive?

Cameron was a real man. He was tough, and he could speak for himself, and he knew how to treat women. Spence was soft-spoken, always overthinking things. He'd rarely seen Anika and Spence together, but he could imagine her bossing him around and dominating him.

Had Anika changed? Was that why Spence loved her? Cameron struggled to see what could make a man love her. Despite her obvious good looks, there was nothing he found particularly interesting in her.

Cameron watched her from his spot near the bar, sipping his drink. She was with a group of her friends, but she didn't look happy. This brought a smile to his face. He didn't know if she was unhappy over Spence, or because she didn't want to be out with her friends, but he intended to find out.

After a while, he got a break when Anika left her friends and went to the bathroom. He waited a few moments, then planted himself nearby. When she emerged, he crossed her path.

'Hey, Nika.'

'Cam?' The shock on her face amused him. There was a moment of intrigue in her eyes, but it was smothered by pain.

After a long look, Anika sighed and tried to step past him. Cameron gripped her wrist, stopping her in place.

'What's your hurry?'

'I don't want to get into it. Least of all with you,' she said.

'You don't have to hide. Spence is working, so you don't have to worry.' Cameron sidestepped her comments.

'I know where my boyfriend is, thanks. Just like he knows I'm out with my friends. Why are you here?'

'Why aren't you with your friends?' Cameron easily avoided the question. Anika was already growing flustered, and he felt more emboldened with every passing moment. Despite the elapsed time, he still knew exactly how to play her.

'I wanted a moment away from them,' said Anika. Cameron nodded.

'You look good.'

Anika shook her head.

'I'm not doing this with you.' She pushed past him and was ready to leave. Cameron already knew how to hook her, though.

'*Fiji.*'

Slowly, Anika faced him. Her eyes met his.

'You always wanted to live in Fiji for a year. You told me about it, way back when. Does Spence know?' Cameron continued.

Anika gritted her teeth. 'Stop it.'

Cameron fought the urge to smile. He had her, and they both knew it.

'No matter what happened with us, I still remember what you said.'

Anika's eyes flared in anger.

'You mean the bits you want to remember. You tend to ignore the rest.' Her eyes watered. 'I don't want to do this with you.'

'I hope you get what you want; what *you* want . . . not you trying to live up to *their* expectations at the expense of your own,' said Cameron, softening his voice. Anika's mouth opened and closed, and then she walked away, returning to her friends.

This time, Cameron didn't stop her. He watched her shut down her friends when they tried talking to her. When she'd had a few more drinks, he sent her a text message.

> Do you ever wish things had turned out differently?

A few seconds later, he sent a second message:

> You don't need to reply. I really do hope you have a good night.

It took a while for him to get a response, but he'd known it would come. Their short conversation had given him significant insight into Anika's mindset. She still cared for him.

> I think about how things could have been, every single day.

Cameron lifted his head up, his phone light casting a sinister light on his face. His smile was wide, creasing the corners of his eyes. He had her right where he wanted. She'd shown her hand, and he knew just how to play it from here.

CHAPTER FIFTEEN

TIME PASSED. Cameron kept working, planning for the future, determined to look good to Rudy and the others. By all accounts, Natty was flourishing in Little London. They were on better terms after arguing about Jaden, but they weren't seeing as much of one another as they had previously.

Tonight, though, Cameron had plans.

Anika was coming to see him. It had taken a while, and he'd begun to assume she wasn't interested, but in the end, Cameron was right; she couldn't resist the temptation.

In terms of preparation, he didn't do much. He tidied the living room, and made sure his drugs stash was healthy, in case she still liked to partake.

When she knocked at the door, he let her in, staring her down. She'd dressed to impress, which he saw as a good sign. She wore a grey skirt and a black top, and her legs seemed longer than he remembered. She sat down, and he fixed her a glass of wine.

'Do you want anything else? I've got pills, coke, or some weed,' Cameron said, noting how stiff she looked. He needed to play this carefully, or she would leave before anything could happen.

They shared a spliff. After finishing her glass of wine, Cameron refilled her drink, noting that she seemed more relaxed now, and was no longer rigidly sitting on the sofa.

'A big part of me knows I shouldn't be here,' she said, after taking another sip of wine.

'Is that why it took you like two weeks to reach out to me?'

Anika cleared her throat.

'I wasn't sure. Like I said . . . I shouldn't be here.'

'You think too much.' Cameron laughed, glancing at her legs. He couldn't wait to fuck her. 'You're here for a reason.'

Anika's eyes narrowed.

'Does everything boil down to sex?'

Cameron swirled his drink around his glass before taking a long sip. Smacking his lips, his eyes fixed on the glass. Eventually, his eyes met hers.

'Why did you finally come to see me?' This was all part of the plan. He wanted her off-balance, making it easier to get what he wanted.

'I want closure.'

'You want freedom, not closure.'

'That probably means getting bent over in your world,' said Anika dryly.

Cameron smirked. She wasn't wrong. The difference was, he knew they both wanted the same thing. He was just more upfront about it.

'I spoke with Natty,' Anika said.

Cameron jerked, spilling his drink. He wasn't expecting that. If Natty knew what he was doing with Anika, he was fucked. Natty wouldn't listen to reason, and it would scupper everything he was working for.

'Shit.' He dabbed at his clothes, scowling. 'Does he know we're talking again?'

'Course not.' Anika shook her head.

Cameron took a deep breath, visibly relieved. He wiped at the stain on his top one last time, then left it. He would need to play this carefully.

'Good. Natty wouldn't understand,' he said.

'How do you know that? He's a gyalist. He'd probably support you.' Anika scoffed.

Cameron shook his head. She didn't get it.

'He and Spence are tight. He'd see anything I did as a violation.'

'Does Natty know how deep things were with us?' Anika asked.

Cameron hesitated before answering, unsure of Anika's angle. He didn't like that she kept bringing up Natty. Eventually, he shook his head.

'That's in the past. He knew we had a little thing, but it doesn't matter anymore.'

Anika froze. After a moment, she drained her drink and poured another.

'Why did you never love me?'

Cameron rubbed his forehead, eyes narrowing. This was the last thing he wanted to get into with Anika. He didn't want her getting too caught up in her feelings.

'How do you know I didn't?'

'If you had, we would have been together.'

'If that's how you felt, you wouldn't have got with my friend.' Cam had landed a blow, and he knew it. Anika blanched, before taking a deep breath.

'Spence cares about me.'

Cameron snorted. Anika was still pretending she cared about Spence, despite the fact she was here with him. It was laughable.

'He's soft,' he finally said.

'You two don't seem to like one another. Why do you still think you're friends?'

Cameron shrugged.

'We're just different. Doesn't mean you should have gone for him, though.'

Anika rubbed her eyes. Cameron could tell she was getting frustrated.

'I never had to guess how Spence feels about me. He tells me and shows me, and he wants to build something with me—'

'Why the hell are you here then?' Cameron snapped, suddenly annoyed with hearing about how perfect Spence was. 'Why sit with me when you can be at home with your perfect fucking boyfriend?'

'Because I don't love him!' Anika screamed. Cameron didn't show it, but he inwardly grinned. They both stared at one another, breathing hard.

'I wish I did. It would be so much easier, but I don't,' Anika finished.

'Who do you love?' Cameron's voice was softer now. This was it. He had her. He just needed to reel her in. Anika shook her head, clearly at war with herself. Cameron moved closer. When she didn't back away, his lips met hers, and she kissed him back.

Later, Cameron wrapped his arm around Anika, a smile on his face. He felt her tracing patterns across his chest, and his smile widened. He'd done it. Despite all of Spence's virtues, the woman he loved wanted Cameron. It was a powerful feeling, and though there was a sliver of guilt, it was ruthlessly quashed.

Now, he needed to plan his next move. Telling Spence what had happened wasn't an option, but he wasn't sure how things could work long-term. They could creep around, but that never lasted. Sooner or later, it would come out.

'Cam?' Anika said.

'You should jet soon. Spence is working, but he might drop in on you. See what you're doing.'

'Spence isn't like that. He trusts me.'

Cameron rolled his eyes. The fact she was there with him was a sign Spence shouldn't trust her. He'd known it all along; under the right circumstances, Anika would cast Spence aside.

An awkward thought crept into his mind.

Was Anika like this when they were together? Was she sleeping with other guys then?

'Still, you don't wanna make him suspicious. Might make it harder to get away next time.'

'Next time?' Anika glanced up at him, frowning when she saw his smile.

'Yes, next time. Save all the hard-to-get shit. You loved what we did. You came like four times.'

'Just because I enjoyed having sex with you, doesn't mean anything has been resolved between us. What is it that you want from me, Cam? Do you want me to stay with Spence?'

'Do you want to?'

Anika didn't reply immediately.

'Spence cares about me,' she repeated. Cameron shifted, but didn't shoot down the answer this time.

'Is caring enough?'

'Can you offer me something more?' Anika countered.

Cameron shrugged. He wasn't committing to anything with Anika. Not anytime soon, anyway.

'I don't know. I guess I'd like to, but that doesn't mean I can.'

Without a word, Anika slid from the bed and began getting her things together. Cameron watched her, arms behind his head, as he savoured her tight body.

'Nika?'

She glanced back at him.

'I'm glad you took a chance with me.'

Anika opened, then closed her mouth.

'I don't know what I'm supposed to say to that,' she said. 'There's a lot I need to think about.'

'I know. Whatever happens, though . . . this was fun, right?'

Anika nodded, giggling.

'You're such a piece of shit,' she said. 'I don't know how you got around me. I'm not supposed to be laughing.'

'Savour it.' Cameron got up, and when Anika was ready, they headed back downstairs. He called her an Uber, pressing her against the living room wall and kissing her some more, pressing his body against hers as she leaned further into the kiss. When the notification from the driver came, he let her go, closing the door behind her and locking it.

Wiping his mouth, his grin deepened, and he went to make a drink. He had a lot to think about.

His reputation in the crew was growing. He was making more money, despite being overlooked by his friend for promotion. Having got the promotion and what he *wanted*, Spence looked set to lose what he *needed*.

Taking a sip of his drink, Cameron smiled as he considered his position. Right now, his life was lovely.

CHAPTER SIXTEEN

CAMERON SAW LESS of Natty as time went on. He was busy in Little London, and Cameron was splitting his time between hustling, and doing jobs for Rudy and Marlon. They were mainly collections, and none of them caused much trouble. Cameron had learned his lesson from dealing with Christian, and ensured he took precautions before doing any pickups.

One minor blip was an incident that happened with Spence. Spence believed that one of their workers, a cocky dude named Gavin, was stealing. Cameron argued against it, believing Gavin was loyal, and a good guy. Rather than take his word for it, Spence had set Gavin up, then confronted him, forcing him to admit he had been skimming.

The whole event made Cameron look stupid, and caused a standoff between him and Spence that Spence won, with the crew members present all supporting him. Cameron lost clout amongst the crew, and even Rudy had sent word through Marlon that he was disappointed that he had allowed himself to be manipulated. Gavin had targeted times when he was on shift to run his scams. He'd given Cameron weed and bottles of brandy as gifts, holding conversations with him, knowing all the while that he was getting one over on him.

The bright side for Cameron was Anika.

As he'd suspected, their dalliance hadn't been a one-time thing, and they'd had sex several more times. After Spence had humiliated him in front of the crew, Cameron had taken great pleasure in sleeping with Anika, content to keep taking out his frustrations with his friend, on his friend's girl.

When he wasn't working or dealing with Anika, Cameron was still discretely looking out for Lodi. He hadn't forgotten that the man had stolen from him, and remained determined to catch him. Despite Philip's repeated belief that Lodi had left Leeds behind, Cameron was sure his greed would win over, and that he would be back.

ONE MORNING, Cameron was in the kitchen, phone to his ear as he made breakfast.

'I'm gonna come and see you soon, mum. I've just been proper busy with work lately. It's hard to get time away.'

'I hope so, Cam. It'll be nice to see you, even if it's just for a little bit. I'm glad things seem to have picked up for you, though.'

'Thanks,' Cameron replied. He'd finally paid his mum back, apologising for taking so long, which had got her off his back. 'I just needed some time to get stuff sorted out.'

'When are you going to sort out getting a girlfriend?'

'Mum . . . don't start that again.' Cameron rolled his eyes, adding some pepper to his eggs. Anika flitted to his mind for a moment, and he tensed.

'You're not getting any younger, Cam. You need to find someone to look after you. Think about your future.'

'I will. I promise. Look, I've gotta go, but I'll speak to you later.'

'Okay, Cam. I love you.'

'I love you too, mum.'

When Cameron had finished his breakfast, he took a shower, again thinking about Anika. It irked him that she kept popping up in his thoughts. He had her back on the string, and that was supposed to be it. He didn't want anything more than that, yet the thought of her spending time with . . . or sleeping with Spence, made him want to break something. He needed to get past it, but wasn't sure how.

Once he was ready, he considered going to the gym, but was still on the sofa watching television an hour later when his phone rang.

'Yeah?'

'Are you home?' It was Rudy. Cameron straightened in his seat.

'Yeah. Something wrong?'

'Come to the office. We're going for a drive.'

CHAPTER SEVENTEEN

RUDY'S EXPRESSION was blank when he climbed into Cameron's car. They greeted one another, then said nothing as Cameron started to drive.

'Where are we going?' Cameron asked.

'I'll get the address now.' Rudy reached for his phone. 'Has everything died down with your work situation?'

'Yeah,' said Cameron, instantly quashing the frustration and embarrassment he still felt. He loathed the fact people were looking down on him over a little mistake.

'Good.' Rudy gave him the address. 'Keep it that way. I don't want you brought down by nonsense. When we get to this meeting, I want you to stay out of the way. Got it?'

'I got it,' replied Cameron, his excitement growing.

They drove to Gipton, and parked on a quiet street. A kid was throwing stones at a wall, pausing when he saw them. He kept his eyes on Cameron, who ignored him. The kid couldn't be more than four years old, but was playing on a street with no one in sight. He didn't get it, but quickly decided it wasn't his problem.

Rudy led the way to a house. It had a peeling white door with a metal shutter on the front and metal bars on the windows. Cameron glanced around, noting a few houses with the same setup.

A scowling brown-haired man answered the door, acknowledging Rudy with a grunt and leading them inside. Their stench of body odour lingered in the air, causing Cameron to put his head down and fight through the smell.

In the living room, a man waited. He had dirty blond hair with a prominent widow's peak, and dark circles under his eyes. He stared at Cameron for a long moment.

'Who's this?'

'He's part of the team,' said Rudy. 'Cam, this is Peter. Peter, Cam.'

Cameron held out his hand, but Peter ignored it.

'You need to tell me when you're bringing new people to me,' he said to Rudy. Rudy's eyebrow rose.

'I don't need to tell you anything. Get that clear in your head, so we don't have this problem again,' Rudy coldly replied. Cameron tensed, wondering if they were going to have to fight their way out. He didn't understand the dynamics, or why there seemed to be so much tension between the pair.

After a moment, Peter shrugged.

'Fine. Whatever. We've got more important shit to deal with, anyway. You said you would deal with Morris and his team, but they're still out there, causing shit for us.'

'I said I'll deal with it, and I will. That doesn't give you the right to hold back profits. You know what you're supposed to pay weekly, and I know you have it. From now on, Cam is going to do the pickup. He's gonna leave you his number, and you're going to get one of your guys to drop off our cut.'

Peter's brow furrowed.

'What about my problem?'

'As I said, it will be handled.'

They spoke for a while longer, but the conversation became more general, and Cameron tuned out. He didn't know the names mentioned, but did wonder who *Morris* was, and what sort of problems he was causing for Peter.

After a while, they left.

'Take me back to Delores's,' said Rudy, pulling out his phone and glancing at the screen.

'Cool,' Cameron replied. He was pleased that he had another job to do for Rudy, one from which he had the opportunity to make new connections. He wondered if Natty knew about Rudy's Gipton connections, but doubted it. As he pulled away, he noted that the kid was still playing by himself, though he'd paused his stone-throwing to watch the car drive away.

'Peter is a liability, but he's an important man in the area,' Rudy said, surprising Cameron. 'He makes our job easier.'

'Even in spite of this Morris guy?' Cameron replied, allowing a car to proceed in front of him before driving on.

'Yeah. Morris is an annoyance, but he's not the big deal Peter is making him out to be. He just likes having something to complain about. Some people are like that.'

Rudy said nothing else, and they drove back to the Hood.

'Have you heard from Nathaniel?' He asked, when they pulled up on Francis Street.

'Nah, he's been busy in Little London. We don't really chill like we used to.'

Rudy looked confused for a moment.

'You were to keep an eye on him, were you not?' He asked.

Cameron nodded.

'I have been when I can. We've just got our own things now. Little London takes a lot of his time, and when I'm not working with Spence, I'm working for you.'

Rudy continued to look at Cameron and, after a moment, nodded.

'It's good he's staying focused. Next time you speak to him, I'd like to hear what he says.'

'Is something wrong?' Cameron asked. He knew Rudy was interested in Natty's welfare, but it seemed strange he didn't reach out himself.

'No.'

That was it. Rudy didn't add anything more, and the subject awkwardly lingered in the air. After a moment, Rudy opened the car door. Pausing, he reached into his pocket and handed Cameron a bundle of notes.

'You did well today. Keep it up.'

'I will. Thanks,' replied Cameron, but Rudy was already walking away.

CHAPTER EIGHTEEN

CAMERON INTENDED to speak with Natty about Rudy's comments, but became distracted by the latest news circling the Hood.

Natty's foray into Little London hadn't sat well with a local gangster named Warren. Warren was the main man in the area, and apparently, peace talks had gone sour between the groups. Warren had escalated the drama further, and now, war was brewing in the streets.

Things ramped up after that. Shots were fired, and people were beaten up on the streets of Little London. When Cameron spoke with Natty, his friend was frustrated over the lack of direct action, stating Rudy was preventing him from going on the attack.

'Why do you think he's doing that?' Cameron asked one night. Natty had driven to his house, and the pair were sat in the car. Natty was smoking a cigarette — his second one since he pulled up. He looked tired and annoyed, but there was also another glow . . . similar to one Cameron noted Spence had.

The glow of a leader.

Despite everything. Despite the moves Cameron was

making, and the additional money coming in, he was still behind his friends, which ate away at him. He wanted more. He wanted to overshadow them, but it just didn't seem possible.

'I don't know. Maybe he doesn't think I could handle it.'

'Could you? Or, would you want to?'

'I just want the situation sorted. It's harder to do business if everyone thinks we're soft. I wouldn't mind if I knew of a plan to resolve the situation, but Elijah and Rudy just want me to sit tight. That doesn't make sense when you're dealing with a man that refuses to do business.'

Cameron listened, but added nothing. Natty was his friend, but more importantly, he was a rival, and Cameron had to consider his own position. He found it ironic Natty was talking about the crew looking soft, when Spence was making *him* soft. In a way, he'd brought it on himself.

Natty left a while later, no closer to a resolution.

Despite his lack of advice, Cameron knew Natty was right. Warren wasn't playing ball, and didn't seem to want to. He needed to die, and someone needed to step up and do it.

A growing part of Cameron wanted to be that person. He wanted the clout. He wanted the respect from people around him as someone that could handle problems. Killing someone was going to the next level, street-wise, and he was sure he could do it.

Doubt ate away at him, though.

You couldn't take back killing someone.

What if it came time to pull the trigger, and he froze?

The whole situation caused him more confusion, and he stopped thinking about it.

DAYS WENT BY, and he met with Peter's people, doing the pickups, and dropping them off on either Marlon or Rudy directly. He told Rudy of Natty's thoughts, but Rudy didn't say much about them, leaving Cameron in limbo.

And then, Warren was dead.

Just like that.

Murdered in a house in Little London, along with some of his closest workers.

It baffled everyone, Cameron included. There were rumblings in the streets that Natty had done the deed, but Cameron knew that wasn't true. He didn't even need to speak to his friend to confirm it. Still, Natty was picked up and questioned by the police, but was released without being charged.

Cameron suspected Rudy had ordered the killing, but Rudy gave nothing away whenever they spoke. Conceding that he would likely never know what truly happened, Cameron resolved to move on and concentrate on his plans.

SOMETIME LATER, Cameron was at a birthday bash in the Hood that his cousin had mentioned. Cameron had gone with his cousin, but they separated shortly after arrival. Cameron was dressed to impress, flossing a new watch and chain he'd bought, along with his all-Gucci outfit. There were a lot of eyes on him as he did the rounds, and he loved the attention.

Soon, he was talking with a woman. They'd posed for a photo and flirted a little bit, and he was considering inviting her back, when someone entered his space. When Cameron realised it was Wonder, he tensed.

'Be easy, bro.' Wonder shook his head. 'There's no hard feelings from that last shit. We're on the same side now.'

Cameron nodded, relaxing. He turned to the woman he'd been talking to.

'Go get yourself a drink, babe. I need to chat to my boy here.'

'She's a baddie,' said Wonder, giving the woman an appreciative glance as she walked away. 'Is that your girl?'

'Nah. Just seeing what I can make happen,' said Cameron. Wonder laughed, then sipped his drink. Cameron understood why Wonder had approached, but didn't understand why he was lingering. They'd said their piece, and established there were no problems between their crews.

What more needed to be said?

'Where's Natty?' Wonder asked.

Cameron shrugged. He hadn't mentioned the bash to either Natty or Spence.

'We don't go everywhere together,' he replied. Wonder chuckled.

'He's probably running around after Raider's kid.'

Cameron almost laughed, remembering how Natty had flipped out on him for upsetting Jaden, but didn't.

'That's my boy you're laughing at.'

'Relax, man. I don't mean any disrespect. We both know that he escalated the situation at Ellie's that time, though. He was ready to fight over nothing.'

Cameron sipped his drink, but didn't comment. Secretly, he wondered if Wonder was right. Natty had been ready to fight a group of people over Lorraine . . . who he claimed to have no feelings for. The same Lorraine whose kid he seemed to enjoy babysitting whenever possible.

Natty and Lorraine were both single. *If their situation was so deep that she trusted Natty with her son, why weren't they taking it further?*

Did he want them to?

Spence and Anika were bad enough. Natty was already changing too much for his liking. Cameron didn't know what to think. As Anika flitted back to his mind, he pushed away the thoughts. He didn't need to think about her anymore tonight. He glanced around, noting the woman he'd been speaking to, was now talking to another guy. His mouth tightened at the disrespect, but he wouldn't cause a fuss.

'Y'know,' Wonder started after a long moment, 'the birthday boy's sister used to deal with Teflon back in the day.'

'Really?' Cameron was impressed. Teflon had been a big deal in the Hood, and was still viewed with respect by many . . . Cameron included. 'Did you ever meet Teflon?'

Wonder shook his head.

'Nah. I saw him in passing once, but you couldn't really get close to him. Elijah used to speak to him, though. Got advice from him and stuff. Those lot were wild, though . . . Shorty, Marcus and that lot.'

Cameron grinned. 'Yeah, they were. Those lot just ran around doing what they wanted, but the streets loved them for it.'

Wonder nodded in agreement. 'They did. Do you think we'll ever get to the same level?'

'I hope so,' said Cameron, looking at Wonder in a new light now. He'd always dismissed him in the past, but he realised now that they had a lot in common.

'Mitch is cool, though. How do you like working for him?'

Cameron scowled, draining his drink, his grip on the glass tightening.

'I don't know Mitch. He's just up there, innit.'

Again, Wonder nodded, taking a sip of his own drink, eyes flitting around the room for a moment.

'I get that. He's Natty's uncle, I suppose. He's the one with the famous surname. I guess he's the one people check for.'

'What are you getting at?' Cameron snapped, annoyed with the subject. 'Mitch is never around. He sits back and collects his money. It doesn't matter if he's Natty's uncle or not.'

'I guess,' said Wonder. 'I'm glad we don't have it like that on our side. Elijah is with us. He breaks bread with the team, and he's in the trenches alongside us.' Again, Wonder glanced around. Cameron followed suit, noting his prospect for the night walking outside with the man she'd started speaking to. 'Little London . . . it's basically a license to print money. Elijah has told us how much we're making. I'm guessing that's what paid for those jewels you're wearing. That Rollie is banging, by the way.'

'Listen, *I* paid for my jewellery,' said Cameron, his tone short. He was annoyed with the talk, and with the fact he'd lost his link for the night. 'Little London is Natty's thing. I don't ask what he's making, and I don't care what he's making.'

Wonder's mouth fell open, his eyes widening.

'You're serious? He's not breaking you off any funds?'

'What did I just say?' Cameron understood now why Natty had been ready to smash a bottle over Wonder's head. He was speaking in circles, and it was frustrating.

'Sorry, fam. I'm not trying to get at you. You just need to consider why you're being left out in the cold, that's all.'

'Stop double talking me,' said Cameron. 'If you have something to say, then just say it.'

Wonder shrugged.

'Look, you're respected in your own right, that's all I'm getting at. People talk about you. You're a thorough motherfucker. I just think Natty might be trying to *son* you, and keep you down.' Wonder glanced past Cameron. 'Shit. I've just seen someone I need to talk to. I've got your number, though. We need to link up soon, fam.' Wonder touched his fist and hurried off. Cameron watched him walk away with a frown, mulling over what he had said.

There was a lot to unpack.

CHAPTER NINETEEN

RUDY WAITED as Elijah and Wonder took their seats. Marlon was on his feet, getting drinks for everyone. Delores had gone to visit her sister, so they didn't have to worry about her disturbing them.

'How are we looking?' He asked.

Elijah nodded.

'Excellent. Things on our end are running smoothly. No hiccups I can think of. Have you made any headway with your contacts?'

Rudy sighed. It was an uphill battle, convincing Mitch's loyalists that there was a better opportunity for them, without directly saying it.

'I'm tempted just to pull the trigger and engineer the coup. Things are moving a little too slowly. Moving along without alerting Mitch is still a struggle, and there's still a wall around him.'

Elijah took a sip of his drink, rubbing his thumb.

'I'd advise you to keep moving as you're doing. It's not like we're standing still. We're still slowly building that war chest in case we *do* need to set it off.'

'I get that,' replied Rudy, but gun for gun, we're never going to be able to meet Mitch on equal footing.'

Elijah shrugged. 'Maybe not. If that's the case, it's even more important to make the right moves, at the right time. I think we need more pieces to keep ourselves insulated.'

'About that . . .' Wonder spoke for the first time, causing the others to look his way. 'Cam is ripe, and ready to be plucked.'

Elijah looked to Rudy, who was surprised by Wonder's words. He hadn't known he was close with Cameron.

'I've given him several jobs to do. He hasn't fucked any of them up. Elijah, what do you think?' Rudy asked.

'I trust Wonder,' replied Elijah. 'As long as we can control him, I'm on board.'

'I'll feel him out. He could be instrumental in bringing Nathaniel on board.'

The atmosphere in the room seemed to shift. Marlon and Wonder shared a look. Rudy's eyes narrowed.

'What?'

Elijah shot Wonder a look, and Wonder sighed.

'Look, Rudy, with all due respect . . . Natty is a psycho. He doesn't like our crew. He's never gonna work with us.'

'He's been working with me in Little London, and he's doing fantastic,' said Elijah.

'Still, he's never gonna play nice with Raider. There's too much bad blood,' Wonder argued.

'Forget it,' interjected Rudy, before Elijah could reply. 'Right now, it doesn't matter. I'll work on cultivating Cameron, and we'll take it from there. Cameron is loyal to clout, and we can get a lot of use out of him.'

―――

A WEEK LATER, Cameron was at Delores's again. Rudy had summoned him, his voice on the phone terser than normal.

Cameron rubbed the back of his neck as he entered, wondering what he could have done. As far as he was concerned, everything was going well. He'd done his collections, including working with Peter's people.

Rudy glanced up when he arrived, smiling at him.

'How's everything going?' He said, signalling for Cameron to sit down. Cameron did so cautiously, having never seen Rudy in such an optimistic mood.

'Everything is good,' said Cameron, still trying to work out what was going on.

'I see you're spending your money.' Rudy studied the chain Cameron was wearing. 'Be careful showing too much of it. You know how the police can be.'

'I know, Rudy. I'm careful, don't worry. Do you need me to do something for you?'

Rudy didn't respond, continuing his evaluation of Cameron. Cameron fought to avoid fidgeting, instinctively understanding that something significant was taking place.

'Do you remember when you picked up the money from Christian for me, the first time?'

Slowly, Cameron nodded.

'Do you remember the conversation we had afterwards?'

'Yeah.'

'You said some things to me that night. You mentioned how much you wanted to develop. You wanted to be the main guy, and you were just waiting for the right opportunity, correct?'

'Yeah, Rudy. That's all true.'

Rudy rubbed his forehead, letting out a sigh.

'Words are different from actions. You talk good, but I'm wondering how down you really are.'

Cameron leaned forward. 'I'm down, Rudy. You know that. I've done as I'm told, and I want to step up. Nah, I'm *ready* to step up. Give me the shot, and let me prove it.'

Again, Rudy surveyed him. Rubbing the underneath of

his chin with his thumb, Rudy took another few seconds, and then spoke.

'I want you to go and see Christian.'

'Okay,' said Cameron, surprised that Rudy had said so much, only to give him a basic task. 'How much does he owe?'

'Christian has . . . had all the chances he's going to get,' said Rudy, meeting Cameron's eyes. It took a second for Cameron to catch on, but his muscles went numb when he did. He felt his lip trembling, and fought to get it under control. Evidently, he hadn't been quick enough. Rudy's eyes narrowed.

'Is that going to be a problem, Cameron?'

Cameron knew without being told that this was it. If he didn't step up now, he would never get another opportunity to do so. Blowing out a breath, he sat straighter in his chair.

'I'll handle it.'

Rudy gave a single nod, rubbing his jaw.

'Marlon will be in touch.'

CHAPTER TWENTY

CAMERON HESITATED. He stood on Christian's street, taking deep breaths, trying to psych himself up. After a minute, he glanced around, checking no one was watching. Finally, he entered the garden and knocked on the door.

Christian answered, warily staring out. Cameron gave him a small smile.

'Are you gonna let me in? You don't want your neighbours to hear our chat, right?' said Cameron. Christian swallowed, then nodded. The living room was unchanged from the last time Cameron had visited. An Xbox One controller rested on the sofa — the video game Christian had been playing currently paused.

'Do you want a drink?' Christian asked.

Cameron shook his head. He felt calmer than he had outside. Something about Christian's nervousness relaxed him.

'I'm good. How have you been?'

Christian's eyebrow rose.

'Why are you asking me that?'

'We used to be cool before that bullshit you pulled. You paid for it, so no reason for me to hold a grudge,' he replied.

'I'm fine.'

'How's your girl?'

Christian scowled, folding his arms.

'We're on a break. She cheated on me.'

Cameron couldn't hide his smirk. Christian noticed.

'It's not funny, mate. I did everything for her, and she violated.'

'It happens. You can't trust women. Next time, you'll know to pick better.' Cameron's thoughts shifted to Anika for a moment. Things in that area didn't seem any easier. 'Anyway, how's business?'

'It's picking up. I've kept my head down, staying out of the mix,' said Christian.

'Yeah?'

'Yeah,' replied Christian. 'I've just been stacking my money. I wanna get out of Leeds as soon as I can.'

Cameron didn't speak for a moment. He wondered whether Rudy would consider the problem solved if Christian moved away. It would certainly save him a lot of trouble, but Cameron doubted it.

It wasn't about the money; it was about the disrespect. Rudy wanted to send a message, and Cameron was the messenger. He cleared his throat.

'You know what, I will have a drink after all.'

'What do you want?'

'Cup of tea. Milk and four sugars.'

Christian headed to the kitchen. Cameron took another deep breath, pulling out the gun Marlon had given him, keeping it by his side. Christian had his back to Cameron, humming a tune.

Cameron stepped towards him.

At the last moment, Christian turned, eyes widening when he saw Cameron. He flung the cup at him, and despite Cameron avoiding the object, it allowed Christian to charge, slapping the gun from his hand. Christian dove for it, but

Cameron kicked him in the side, then punched him twice, his fist crashing against the side of Christian's head. Despite clearly being stunned, Christian let out a roar and charged Cameron, slamming him into a nearby table.

They fell to the floor, Christian mounting Cameron, hitting him twice. Cameron rolled over, overpowering Christian, hands wrapping around his throat. His teeth gritted, watching him attempt to break free. Tighter, he squeezed, wanting it to end. He couldn't afford to fail. His whole future rested on this. If Christian got away, he would stay at the bottom of the ladder his whole life.

Cameron couldn't have that. He *wouldn't* have that.

Christian attempted to claw Cameron's face, trying to break free, but he held on tightly, feeling Christian's strength fade. After a few more seconds, he let go, crawling for the gun. Clambering to his feet, he pointed the gun at Christian's head, hesitating for only a moment before pulling the trigger three times.

Glancing at the dead body for only a moment, Cameron hurried from the house, gun by his side. He kept his head down, striding down the road, taking a left onto the street where he'd parked a stolen getaway car. Climbing in, he drove away at moderate speed.

After five minutes, he stopped the car, opened the door, and threw up.

When he was finished, he carried on driving.

―――

CAMERON STOPPED to see Marlon at a pre-arranged spot, down a secluded backstreet. Marlon climbed out of his car when he saw Cameron. He had two men with him. Both were older, wearing black outfits similar to Cameron's. They looked like they could handle themselves, and for a terrifying moment, Cameron thought they were there to kill him.

'Is it done?' Marlon asked.

Cameron nodded, the image of Christian's dead body returning to his mind.

'Good. These lot are gonna handle the clean-up . . . if no one's called the police, anyway. Are you okay?'

'Yeah . . . I'm fine,' said Cameron, though he felt anything but.

'I get it,' said Marlon, and Cameron finally detected a level of respect in his voice. 'Rudy will contact you directly. Relax until then. Have a stiff drink, and don't tell anyone what you did.'

'I won't,' said Cameron.

'Before that, take those clothes off, and we'll dispose of them. I've got a tracksuit for you in the car.'

Cameron hesitated for a moment, then undressed whilst leant against the car, surprised he hadn't thought about his clothes. Evidently, Marlon and the heavies he had with him were far more used to cleaning up these sorts of messes. The shock he felt over what he'd done, hadn't abated, and he didn't even remember saying goodbye to Marlon after he dressed.

When Cameron got home, he took a shower, then fixed a stiff glass of brandy, downed it, and poured another, wincing. He wanted to drown in alcohol, not wanting to think about what he'd done, yet unable to keep it from his mind. He'd known Christian. Despite his flaws, he wasn't a bad guy, but Cameron had ended his life . . . just so he could get ahead. As he drank, he thought of Christian's ex; whether they would have stayed broken up. He wondered how she would feel when she learned of Christian's death.

Taking a deep breath, he closed his eyes.

Cameron remained despondent when he finally went to see Rudy two days later. He'd spent the time in a drunken, cocaine-fuelled haze, needing the escape from his thoughts. He'd almost called Anika to come and see him, but had called an old link instead.

When Cameron entered Delores's kitchen, Rudy waited, dressed as casually as ever, with a newspaper and an empty mug by his side. It was so familiar that it made Cameron's head spin for a moment. He had killed a man, but the world had continued, as if it never happened.

He wondered if he would ever feel normal again.

Rudy studied Cameron for a long time, as was becoming a habit.

'I spoke with Marlon. He confirmed it was done. How are you feeling?'

'I'm fine,' said Cameron. To his surprise, Rudy shook his head.

'You don't need to front, Cam. I've been in your shoes, and I know what it takes to pull the trigger . . . especially on someone you know.'

There was a quiet pause where neither spoke. Cameron observed Rudy, staring past him in a trance-like state. Shifting awkwardly, Cameron sighed, feeling his shoulders slump.

'I thought it would be easier than it was,' he admitted.

Rudy nodded.

'It's like that. I get it. You did it, though. You proved you have what it takes.' Rudy's expression hardened. 'Before we take the next step, I need full loyalty, no questions asked. If you don't think you can do that, leave and don't come back.'

'I'm in,' said Cameron instantly. He had killed Christian so he could ascend. If he didn't do that, it was all for nothing. He couldn't allow that to happen.

Nodding, Rudy slid to his feet, rummaging around in a cupboard as Cameron watched. He took out a bottle of brandy, and a glass, and poured a drink, handing it to Cameron.

'Coke?'

Cameron shook his head.

'Are you sure? I heard you like brandy and coke.'

'This is fine, thanks,' said Cameron. He'd been drinking brandy without a mixer all weekend. This wouldn't hurt him. He sipped his drink as Rudy sat back down.

'I've worked for Mitch for a long time,' Rudy started. 'I've been proud to do it, and for a long time, things went the right way. Even during the dark times in Leeds, our team always stayed strong. Always stayed loyal. We moved in the right direction.' Rudy glanced down at his newspaper, then back to Cameron. 'Lately, Mitch has lost his way. I don't expect you to understand. You don't know him. You've probably never seen him — not without Nathaniel around, anyway. He's going to bring the whole crew down, and I'm not indicating it's his intent. Regardless, it's going to happen, unless we do something.'

Cameron's throat was dry, hanging on Rudy's every word. He cleared his throat, the brandy in his hand forgotten.

'I didn't realise things were that bad.' He thought about his words with Wonder at the birthday party a while back; he'd said then that he didn't know Mitch. This proved it.

Rudy nodded.

'Panic isn't good for any business. We put a positive spin on everything, and try to keep it all humming. Ventures like Little London are good for us, and they're bringing in much-needed revenue. We need to take over more spots, but Mitch isn't willing to do it. By doing that, he stops people like you, Cam — people more than capable of being leaders — from getting their shot.'

Cameron didn't know what to say. The whole conversation made him nervous, and he knew that there was no going back. The price was too high. His path into this conspiracy had been paid in blood, and he would never be able to escape.

'Elijah and I are working together.'

Rudy's next bombshell brought Cameron back to earth, his hand jolting, almost spilling his drink.

'You can't be fucking serious,' he exclaimed.

'I needed an ally,' replied Rudy, unbothered by Cameron's outburst. 'For all his flaws, Elijah is good at what he does, and he sees the big picture. Action needs to be taken, if we're going to keep our spot at the top of the table. We've been slowly gathering support, and the change is coming.' Again, Rudy paused. 'You've earned the right to be part of that.'

As Cameron sat and pondered these words, Rudy lifted the newspaper, revealing a stack of money. He slid it across to Cameron, who opened his mouth to thank him. Rudy shook his head.

'Don't. You more than earned this with the job you did. Take a couple of days off to think about things. Consider everything we're going to achieve, as a unit.'

CHAPTER TWENTY-ONE

CAMERON SPENT TIME ASSESSING THINGS. The conversation with Rudy had been revealing in a lot of ways. Even in his distorted state, he realised what a risk Rudy had taken in bringing him on board. Sipping liquor, he envisioned being Rudy's right-hand man. There would be no shadow cast over him. Natty and Spence would work for him and Rudy, or they wouldn't work at all.

For once, it would be Cameron leading the way and giving orders.

One thing did strike him, and that was the fact that Rudy hadn't mentioned Natty. He didn't understand why. Rudy cared about Natty — or at least, he appeared to. He was seeing Natty's mum, and he was always acting like Natty's dad. *Why would he leave him out of his scheme?*

Unless he didn't believe Natty would go along with it.

The more Cameron considered this, the more it made sense. Natty cared about his surname. He was happy to be a Dunn, and didn't have a problem working for his uncle; he just wanted to be promoted.

At least, Cameron thought he did. It was harder to get a read on Natty nowadays. He seemed calmer; far more confident in his own skin. An air of quiet confidence seemed to exude from him now. Cameron assumed this was down to the clear success he was having in Little London, and the boost it had given Natty's reputation.

Going to the bathroom to freshen up, he decided to call some company. Again, he considered Anika. The sex was still amazing, but they always ended up talking about emotional stuff, and he found it draining. With everything he had going on, it was the last thing he wanted to deal with.

With that in mind, he called Maxine.

'I can't believe you're just calling me out of the blue again,' she said.

'Still answered, though . . . didn't you?'

'Whatever, Cam. What do you want? I'm back with my man.'

'You wouldn't have answered the phone if he was with you. Pass through and see me for a bit.'

'Are you serious?' Maxine said, her tone incredulous. 'Did you hear what I said?'

'I did. Did you hear what I said? You know what this is. That's why you answered.'

Maxine was silent for a moment. Cameron adjusted the phone, tilting his head and cradling it on his shoulder so he could pick up his drink. He'd taken a long sip when Maxine finally responded.

'I'm only coming because I know you'll have good weed. I'll see you soon.'

Hanging up, Cameron chuckled to himself. Finishing his drink, he swigged some mouthwash and tidied his bedroom. It wouldn't take long for them to end up there.

―――

Later, Cameron lit a spliff after catching his breath. Maxine was still on her stomach, breathing hard. As Cameron inhaled the potent smoke, he watched as she brushed her hair out of her face and turned to look at him.

'How long have you been back with your man?' He asked.

'A while. Don't pretend you care, Cam. Give me a minute to straighten up, and I'll be out of your hair.'

'You don't have to hurry out,' said Cameron. For some reason, he really wanted her company tonight. When he wasn't alone, he didn't think about Christian, or dream about his dead body. It wasn't as bad as the night he'd killed him, but he struggled to move past it. Maxine's eyebrows rose. She rolled over and sat up, smirking at him.

'That's not like you. Usually, you can't wait to get rid of me. What's going on?'

'Nothing. Guess it's just one of those nights.'

'If you say so,' said Maxine. 'Have you got a girlfriend yet?'

'Why would I?' Cameron asked, again thinking of Anika; *the time she'd screamed that she didn't love Spence. The time she all-but admitted she wasn't over Cameron. He closed his eyes.*

'You might get lonely. I don't know. It's not the weirdest thing in the world. How's Natty? I heard he had a girlfriend.'

'You heard wrong. Natty's single like me.'

'What about whats-her-name? *Lorraine?* The one with the little boy. Aren't they together?'

'No, they're just cool. Don't worry about Natty. He's good, and I'm good. In fact, I'm better than good. I'm killing it lately.'

Cameron felt sick as soon as the words left his lips. This was life for him now; random words taking him right back to Christian's living room. Taking a deep breath, he composed himself.

'Oh?' Maxine's eyes widened, her intrigue clear. 'What's going on?'

'I've got big plans,' Cameron said. 'There's big things

going on in the streets, and I'm gonna be right there at the top when it's all said and done.'

'What exactly are you going to be doing?' Maxine asked. Her intrigue appeared to have shifted into concern, and Cameron wasn't sure what to think about that.

'Don't worry,' he finally said. 'It's nothing I can't handle.'

―――――

A FEW DAYS LATER, Cameron and Anika were together again. They had a routine of smoking, having a few drinks, then going to have sex. Cameron noted that she grew more clingy afterwards, not wanting to be away from him, and he liked it. He liked the fact he was getting one over on his friend. He spent little time with Spence when they weren't working, though, and chilled with Natty just as rarely these days.

The main conflict was that the idea of being in a serious relationship still scared him. Anika was cool, as much as she annoyed him from time to time, but it was still daunting to consider taking things further.

'What's on your mind?' Anika asked.

'Just thinking about the future,' Cameron admitted. Anika shuffled closer to him.

'What about it?'

'Nothing deep. Just wondering what might happen.'

'With us?'

'In general.' Cameron shot her a look. She was so pushy at times.

'Fine. I was just asking, Cam. God.'

There was the flip side, Cameron thought, watching her pout. He couldn't deal with the emotional mood swings.

―――――

CAMERON WAS PACING his living room the next day. Natty had called, saying he was coming to speak to him. He hadn't elaborated on why, and that caused Cameron to panic, wondering if Natty had heard about Christian, or about Rudy, or about the seemingly half dozen other things he was hiding from everyone.

Taking a deep breath, he willed himself to calm down. Going to wash his face and sharpen up, he returned downstairs, just as the door opened and Natty walked in, nodding at him. He seemed the same as ever, his solid build and height imposing. His eyes seemed different. Sharper somehow, but with small bags underneath, suggesting late nights and little sleep.

Cameron knew the feeling.

'You look tired,' he said. Natty grinned his agreement.

'I'll be alright. Pity your shit coffee won't do anything for me.'

Cameron laughed. They went to the living room. Natty glanced at the huge television Cameron had bought with his side earnings, his eyebrows raising.

'When did you get that?' He asked.

'I can't remember. A few weeks ago, I think.'

'You have a family member die or something? You're spending money like you own Amazon.'

Cameron chuckled to hide his unease. He didn't want Natty thinking about the money he was making. It would lead to too many questions that he couldn't answer.

'I'm just being better with my money. Maybe Spence is having more of an influence on me than we thought.'

That got a smile out of Natty.

'Maybe. I've noticed I'm not spending as much lately,' he admitted, but continued before Cameron could enquire why. 'Spence is the reason I'm here, anyway.'

'What's happened?'

'Anika.'

Cameron froze, fighting to stay neutral. *There was no way Natty could know.*

'What about her?' He was pleased his voice sounded normal.

'I think she's creeping.'

The bad feeling in the pit of Cameron's stomach grew. He coughed into his fist.

'I'm thirsty. Do you want a drink?' He asked, motioning to the empty glass on the table.

'I'm good,' Natty replied. Cameron topped up his drink, taking advantage of the moment to formulate his responses, prepared to blame it all on Anika if it came up.

'Right,' he started, sipping his brandy to fortify his nerves, 'what were you saying about whats-her-name?'

Natty kept his eyes on Cameron, arms folded across his chest. His expression was grim, causing Cameron to grow ever more nervous. Issues with his friends aside, Natty could more than handle himself, and he didn't want to fight him. Not unless he absolutely had to.

'Back in the day, you lot had your thing . . .' he finally said.

'. . . That's old news. What about it?' said Cameron quickly.

'You know her better than I do. What was she like back then?'

Cameron's mind whirred as he formulated a response. Natty knew something. He didn't realise it was Cameron, but he knew Anika was messing around with someone.

'What have I missed?' He asked after a moment, still trying to gain control of the situation. Natty continued to stare him down as Cameron fought to stay calm.

'Back in the day, you lot had your thing. Do you remember her checking for any other guys in the ends?'

Cameron scratched his chin, needing the extra seconds. The time back then was a blur, but the vibe with Anika was heated from the beginning. He couldn't remember her sniffing around other guys, nor could he think of a patsy he could use to potentially divert suspicion from himself.

'Nah. She liked to go out, and I'm guessing she had connections in the Hood, even back then.'

'What makes you say that?' Natty said.

'She just seemed comfy,' replied Cameron. 'You know the rep Chapeltown has sometimes. Seems scary to people outside of the bubble, but she was always calm.'

Natty didn't respond, still deep in thought.

'Why do you think she's creeping?' Cameron pressed. He needed to know precisely what Natty had.

'She's been acting funny for a while. Saying she's going to see friends, but going somewhere else. I caught her leaving the other night. She took a taxi to the Hood, but I lost track of her at some lights.'

'For real? That's mad.' Panic warred with fury in Cameron's mind. He couldn't believe Anika had been so stupid with her excuses and attitude. She was going to his house that night; he was sure of it. He dreaded to think what would have happened if Natty followed her all the way.

'I'm gonna find out who she's dealing with. Then, I'm gonna deal with them. No one fucks with my people,' said Natty.

'I get it, Nat,' said Cameron, unease growing at Natty's words. He didn't doubt he meant them. 'What do you need from me?'

'Just keep an eye on things. If anyone says anything about Anika or Spence, I wanna hear about it. If anyone is bragging about a new ting they're banging, I wanna hear about it. Cool?'

'Cool, Nat. Spence is my brother too. We'll deal with this.' The words were harder for Cameron to say than he'd imagined, which was worrying.

Was the gulf between him and Spence really so deep?

Natty and Cameron hung out for a while longer, before

Natty's phone rang, and he left. Cameron locked the door behind him, his mind whirring. Natty was relentless when it came to investigating matters like this. He wouldn't stop until he found something, and if he interrogated Anika, it would end badly for both of them.

Cameron stomped back to the living room and grabbed his phone, needing to have words with her.

CHAPTER TWENTY-TWO

AS SOON AS Anika approached the front door, Cameron quickly answered, dragging her inside and locking the door behind them. Anika jerked her arm away, glaring.

'What the hell are you doing?'

'I could ask you the same damn question,' Cameron snapped, needing her to know how mad he was. He noted a flash of worry in her eyes, followed by a frown.

'What do you mean?'

'Natty came to see me.'

Anika's mouth fell open.

'Why?'

'Because he thinks you're cheating on Spence.'

Anika swayed in place, then took several deep breaths.

'Why does he think that?'

'Because you have no fucking chill,' Cameron snarled. 'What the hell is going on between you and Spence?'

'What do you mean?' Anika repeated.

'Natty says Spence thinks you've changed. He's seen you getting all dressed up, and Natty knows you're not going to your stupid friend's house. He even followed you to the Hood . . . the last time you came here.'

'What?' Anika gasped, flinching. 'How does he know all of that?'

'Because he's smart,' Cameron roared, furious that she didn't get it. 'He put it together, and now he's asking me questions about you; about dudes you might know in the Hood.'

'What did you say to him?' Anika's voice shook. Cameron's eyes narrowed.

'What the fuck do you think I said? What was I supposed to say? I said I would ask around.'

Neither spoke for a moment, gathering their thoughts.

'Well?' Cameron finally demanded, needing more from her.

'Well, what?'

'What is going on with you and Spence?'

'Nothing,' she snapped. 'We're barely communicating, but that doesn't mean —'

'What? Doesn't mean he should speak to his friend and tell him you're different? Use your damn brain. Spence is too smart for his own good, and Natty is sharp. He sees the things Spence doesn't.'

Anika took another deep breath, exhaling.

'What do we do now?'

Cameron rubbed his forehead, sighing.

'We keep it calm. You need to fix your relationship and stop Spence suspecting anything. Doesn't matter how you do it . . . listen to Spence talk about his day, or sit and watch Netflix. It just needs containing. If that happens, he'll tell Natty it's calm, and things will return to normal.'

'Okay. What happens after that?'

Cameron didn't know what to say. He wondered why he was fighting so hard to keep this going with Anika. He'd gotten her back, even when she was in a serious relationship with his friend. She'd succumbed to him multiple times.

So, why was he continuing it?

HUSTLER'S AMBITION

———

As time passed, Cameron found himself putting the Anika situation to the side, more focused on everything else going on. When he wasn't hustling, he spent more time around Marlon and Wonder, discussing future steps.

As well as paying him for jobs, Rudy was also giving him additional money, calling it a taste of things to come.

On this particular night, Cameron was having an evening to himself, hanging out and playing on his Xbox. He was tempted to ignore his phone when it rang, but when he saw Rudy's number, he knew that wasn't possible.

He wasn't Natty. He wouldn't get away with blanking Rudy.

'Everything good?' He answered.

'Get to Delores's. Now.'

Rudy hung up. Cameron stared at the phone, his heart racing. Rudy could be extremely curt and direct, but he had never sounded as deadly as he had just then. Cameron freshened up, rubbed his clothes with a lint roller, then headed out.

When he arrived at Delores's home, Elijah and Wonder were also present. The first thing Cameron noticed was that Elijah's usually affable demeanour had vanished. He looked furious, eyeing Cameron with extreme dislike, which startled him. Elijah had been cool with him the few times they had been around one another, so the sudden vitriol was jarring.

Cameron faced Rudy, whose nostrils flared. He looked both enraged and highly stressed out. Cameron didn't know what had happened, but it was serious.

'Did you have anything to do with it?' Rudy demanded, as Cameron remained standing, the eyes of the trio on him.

Cameron didn't have a clue what they were talking about. His bemusement evidently showed on his face, because Rudy spoke again.

'Do you know what happened?'

Cameron shook his head.

'I've been at home chilling. Haven't really spoken to anyone today.'

Elijah growled, and Wonder shook his head.

'Raider was found earlier, badly beaten up in his house. He's in hospital, but it's touch and go,' said Rudy.

Cameron felt his eyes widen. Raider was among the toughest in the streets of Chapeltown. To hear about him being hospitalised was a shock. Immediately, he suspected Natty was behind the attack. Not many could get the better of Raider, and Natty definitely had enough about him to have orchestrated it.

He didn't know how or why, but he was sure Lorraine was involved.

'Did Natty do it?'

The trio shared a look, then Rudy spoke again.

'Have you heard from him?'

Cameron shook his head. A sense of urgency surged through him. Natty's stock had been rising for a long time, and Cameron had struggled to keep up with him. It seemed the tables were turning. With Cameron ascending at Rudy's side, it seemed like an opportunity to overtake his friend, and that feeling was intoxicating.

'I told you he was a problem, Rudy. Numerous times. I told you he couldn't be tamed,' Elijah said, his eyes hard and teeth clamped together. 'Your stepson is an animal; wild and reckless. For all your experience and wisdom, you've got this one badly wrong.'

Rudy and Elijah held each other's stare for a long moment, the others in the room shifting nervously.

'If he's the one that attacked Raider, it has to be about Lorraine, right?' Cameron said, breaking the silence.

Rudy looked from Elijah to Cameron, who was gratified to see the look of approval on his mentor's face.

'I want him dead. Tonight.'

The room fell silent. Cameron held his breath in anticipation of how Rudy would respond. The stress on Rudy's face seemed to have deepened in the last few minutes, and Cameron couldn't help wondering what was going through his mind.

'We can't kill him. Mitch won't allow that.'

'Fuck Mitch!'

Cameron had never heard Elijah sound so unglued. Rudy's jaw tightened.

'Stop being emotional. Remember the plan. We can't jeopardise that, and you know it.'

Elijah shook his head, but argued no further. Wonder shot Cameron a look, but didn't add anything either.

Cameron frowned as he mulled over Rudy's words, annoyed at his handling of the situation. The dynamics of his relationship with Natty seemed to be affecting business. Cameron believed Rudy was trying to protect Natty, despite him putting everything they had worked so hard for at risk.

It took Cameron back to his previous thoughts about his friends; It was clearer than ever that their positions had been given, not earned. Natty had badly overstepped, but Rudy seemed willing to give him a pass, not because of his value to the crew, but because of his name. Regardless, it meant little to Cameron. He'd gone about it the hard way, but he'd earned every opportunity. He was making the right moves, and his friends were floundering.

They should have known better.

Cameron cleared his throat, drawing the attention of the room.

'I'll speak to Natty, and see what he's saying,' he told them. Rudy nodded, but no one else said anything. As Cameron left, he noted Wonder was following. He opened the front door and headed outside.

'We need to have a chat.'

'Okay. I'll get at you later on.'

'Cool. I'll be about.'

Cameron climbed in his car and drove away, wondering what Wonder wanted to discuss.

Later, Wonder climbed into Cameron's car. They were parked on Markham Avenue in the Hood, the street fairly busy, with children playing, and people walking up and down the road, going about their business.

'Thanks for meeting me,' said Wonder.

'I was curious,' said Cameron. 'There's a lot going on right now.'

'You're telling me. That shit with Natty is nuts. He nearly killed Raider, man. Like, if people hadn't found him, he'd have probably died in his house.'

'That's mad,' admitted Cameron. 'Elijah would have definitely tried killing Natty then.'

Wonder tilted his head. 'You've changed, fam. You've stepped your game up. I've noticed it lately when I've seen you. Even in the room earlier, you were confident, and you looked like a boss. I wasn't the only one that noticed.'

'Thanks, bro. I appreciate that.' Cameron hid a smile, ecstatic he was finally being noticed for his skills.

'What do you think about what happened?'

Cameron scratched his chin.

'I think Rudy is protecting Natty.'

Wonder shot him another look of approval, showing that was the answer he had been looking for.

'I told Elijah that you were smart. He wasn't happy about what he heard earlier, and doesn't like Rudy's position.'

'He still took it, though. He backed down from wanting Natty dead,' Cameron pointed out.

'For now.'

Cameron's heart hammered against his chest. Wonder was

blatantly talking about killing Natty, and he wasn't sure how to feel about it.

Wonder continued.

'We work with Rudy because we have to. For now. I wanted to speak with you to tell you that you should think long-term about what you want to do, because Rudy doesn't have our best interests at heart.' He paused, studying Cameron's face. 'You do, though. Think about that.'

Cameron opened his mouth, then closed it, determined to do as Wonder suggested, his mind alight with all the possibilities. Rudy had been good to him, but going after Mitch was a huge deal, and if he was too focused on protecting Natty, then maybe Cameron taking over was the best thing to do.

Not only that, it put Cameron one step closer to being the main guy on the streets of Leeds.

'Like I said, just think about it,' Wonder repeated.

CHAPTER TWENTY-THREE

THE NEXT DAY, Cameron worked his shift in a buoyant mood. People were already speculating on Raider's attack and who was behind it, but Cameron refused to be drawn into the discussions. It amused him watching people hypothesise. He considered himself above it now.

Despite his words to Rudy, he'd intentionally not spoken to Natty. The rumours circling were outlandish. That was useful to Cameron. As the tale passed from person to person, Natty's stock took more of a hit. He would find out in the end and report back to Rudy, but there was no rush.

Opening his door and kicking his trainers off, Cameron dug into his pocket and pulled out his phone. Reading a text from Anika, he responded, placed his phone back in his pocket and made his way upstairs to freshen up.

When Anika arrived, he'd already had a few drinks. He was determined to concentrate on the good things in his life. On the whole, he was in a good place, and he was determined to celebrate that. His conversation with Wonder and his task to speak to Natty were problems for another day and, if he drank enough, he was sure his mind would grant him a restful sleep.

'You look like you're in a good mood,' Anika commented, eyebrows raised as she watched him making her a drink. Handing her the glass, Cameron pulled her close, his lips meeting hers in a scorching kiss. By the time he let her go, some of his drink had spilled on his jumper, but he didn't care.

He could always buy another.

The evening with Anika was one of the best Cameron could remember. They drank and smoked and had sex multiple times.

For the first time in a long time, Cameron felt truly happy. He was walking on air, elated that after so many setbacks, things were finally coming good.

―――

The next day, Cameron was startled by someone banging on his door. Grumbling, he went to answer, shocked when he saw Natty standing there.

'Couldn't you have called before you turned up?' He said, disguising his surprise behind a scowl.

'What's the big deal? Are you busy?' said Natty. Cameron noted with delight that Natty seemed extremely downtrodden and showed some bruising on his face. Despite this, though, there was a fire in his eyes that surprised Cameron.

He wondered if this was what Rudy saw in his friend.

'Nah, nothing like that. You just knock like you're fucking police.'

'Whatever. Move out the way and let me in.'

They headed for the kitchen. Cameron fixed himself a coffee, hoping Anika had the sense to stay quiet. He offered to make one for Natty, but he declined.

'Figured I'd hear from you. Streets are saying some shit about Raider. Was that you?'

Natty nodded. Cameron shook his head, laughing.

Everyone knew, but it was nice to have it confirmed. He would also be able to go back to Rudy with confirmation.

'You nearly killed him. What made you go off like that on him?'

Natty filled Cameron in. Cameron was shocked that Raider had beaten up Lorraine. His suspicions had been correct, though. He'd suspected she was involved.

'You're playing a dangerous game, Nat. Raider's a prick, but he's Elijah's boy. He can't lose face on this one. What if he snitches on you?'

'I don't know, Cam.' Natty rubbed his eyes. 'I tried calling Elijah beforehand to get Raider's details, but he didn't answer. I wasn't gonna wait.'

Cameron sipped his drink, remembering his meeting with Rudy and the others. He had information Natty didn't, along with a direct line to upper levels. The feeling of power was exhilarating.

'I always knew you were whipped over her,' he finally said, unable to resist getting a shot in.

Both men shared a look, then instantly began laughing. It was such a random response to a serious situation, but Cameron couldn't help it.

'This isn't about that. He beat her up for no reason, and I wasn't gonna take that,' said Natty, when they recovered.

'Big difference between smacking someone around and nearly killing them.' The image of Christian slumped on the floor flashed into Cameron's mind. He felt himself flinch, but quashed it. He was past that now. He wasn't going to live in fear and regret his whole life.

Natty shrugged, not giving much away.

'At least you didn't kill him. I'm surprised you didn't.'

Natty frowned. Cameron didn't know why, and before they could discuss further, Natty changed the subject.

'It doesn't matter now. Did you handle that thing?'

'What thing?' Cameron was nonplussed, unable to remember Natty asking him to do anything.

'Anika. Did you learn anything?'

'Oh . . . Nah. If she's creeping with someone in the Hood, she's keeping it lowkey.'

'Spence is out of town, so I figured this would be the time for her to link her dude on the side. If I didn't have all this going on, I'd watch the house to see where she went.'

'Leave it with me, bro,' said Cameron, not letting on just how close Natty was in his assessment. 'I'll look into it some more. You've got enough on your plate.'

'Okay. I appreciate it. Ring me if you hear anything.' Natty touched fists with Cameron, then left.

Cameron locked the door behind his friend. Staring into space for a moment, he gathered himself and headed back upstairs.

Anika sat on the edge of the bed, pulling on her clothes. She glanced up at Cameron.

'Who was that?'

'Natty.' Cameron paced the bedroom. Natty wasn't going to let the situation slide. Anika was on his radar. 'He was asking about you.'

'He knows I'm here?' Anika jumped to her feet, panicking.

'Course not. If he knew, he'd have dragged you out of the house.'

'And you'd let him do that?'

The pair locked eyes. Cameron was struck dumb by her beauty for a moment. They'd had a great night, but it seemed less important now. When it came down to it, he couldn't have Anika messing things up for him. Not now, when he was so close.

'We need to stop this.'

Anika's mouth fell open. Cameron could see her struggling to compose herself.

'What?'

'It's getting on top now. Natty ain't gonna stop until he finds something, and we're getting sloppy. You shouldn't have stayed the night. We should have done this after he first came to me.'

'You . . . you can't be serious. What about everything we have? Everything you said to me?' Anika's eyes were wide, her mouth trembling. Cameron fought down his reluctance. He couldn't let Anika stand in the way of his ascension.

'We got sloppy,' he repeated. 'You have a man, and I'm not waiting around for things to come out. We need to end it now.'

'I can't . . .'

Cameron held up a hand, losing patience with her. Anika wasn't seeing what was right in front of her. She was cheating on her man, and now they were at risk of being discovered. He wouldn't allow her to mess things up for him.

'It's over. And let me tell you right now, don't let me hear about you saying anything to anyone.'

Anika's eyes widened, and he knew she understood.

'You're threatening me?'

'Only if you're dumb enough to call my name. Don't put me to the test. Even if anyone says anything, you'd better make something up. Got it?'

Anika stared at him.

'I said, *got it*?' Cameron took a step forward, and Anika flinched, the fear palpable. She nodded. Gathering her things, she hurried from the house without a word.

Cameron sighed. He'd allowed himself to get too close, but he had fixed it in the end.

Collapsing onto his sofa, he built a spliff, needing to relax. There were more important things to focus on.

CHAPTER TWENTY-FOUR

RUDY WAITED in the cellar of another safe house, smoking a cigarette, awaiting Nathaniel's arrival. The cellar had been converted over the years, and was large enough for Rudy to be able to pace the room. He'd hoped Nathaniel would come to him of his own volition, but he hadn't, and Rudy had been forced to get him. As Nathaniel was led down the cellar steps toward him, Rudy's annoyance grew further.

The look on Nathaniel's marred face didn't make things any better. There was no guilt or worry, only defiance.

They were left alone, and Rudy finished his cigarette, aware of the mounting tension. He was sure Nathaniel would break it by speaking first, but he didn't.

'What the hell were you thinking?' Rudy started. Nathaniel opened his mouth, but Rudy raised his hand, and he immediately fell silent. 'You've jeopardised an alliance, undone months of hard work with your stupid stunt.'

'That wasn't the intention, Rudy. Raider beat up his baby mum, knowing full well what I would do.'

'I don't care about that,' said Rudy, his scowl deepening. He couldn't believe Nathaniel had allowed his emotions to get the better of him. Over a woman, no less. A woman whose child did not belong to him. 'This is real life. Not television. You involved yourself in a situation you didn't need to be in. You didn't think about the bigger picture; the effects your actions would have on the wider scheme. Now, you've fucked everything up. If Raider doesn't recover, we'll need to make it right with Elijah. He's out for blood.'

Rudy expected Nathaniel to be contrite, but once again, Nathaniel subverted his expectations. His eyes narrowed, and he glared at Rudy as if it was *he* who had done wrong.

'You may not care about the situation, and Elijah may not, but *I* do. Raider overstepped the mark, and you lot weren't going to deal with him. So, I did.'

Both men stared at the other, Nathaniel's defiance only increasing. Rudy was almost impressed with his demeanour, but shook his head. He stepped closer to Nathaniel, almost nose-to-nose with him, looking him dead in the eye.

'You were doing so well, Nathaniel. For a while, we thought you could do it. We thought you could ascend to that next level, but you've undone all that hard work. You're out.'

Natty frowned.

'Out of what?'

'You're gone from the crew. Effective immediately. We don't want to see you at any of the spots. You'll be paid up to date, and that's it.'

Nathaniel froze, and Rudy knew with a relish that the impacts of his actions were finally clear. Nathaniel cleared his throat.

'I . . . let me talk to my uncle. I can fix this.'

'There's nothing to say, and nothing to fix. The man you came with will escort you out. Goodbye, Nathaniel.'

Rudy watched with a smile as Nathaniel was escorted from the room. He was sure he could still save this, in the long run. Once Mitch was out of the way, he would have more time to work on manipulating Nathaniel. As long as he stayed out of Elijah's way, and spent his time thinking about his actions, it would be good for him.

Rudy took a deep breath, his mind at work, thinking of the angles; whether he had missed anything. He needed to speak to Mitch, and at least make him aware of the situation.

He would leave out that he had kicked Nathaniel from the crew, though. There was no reason for Mitch to know that.

The ignorance would only further aid their cause, Rudy thought with a smile.

THINGS WERE quiet over the next few days. Cameron knew Natty was out of the crew, but no one was saying much else. He hadn't spoken with Wonder since their last conversation, but had filled in Rudy on what Natty had said, though much to his chagrin, Rudy already knew it all.

Cameron found himself antsy, waiting for something to happen. He had expected Elijah to go for Natty, regardless of Rudy's warnings, but he didn't.

The anticipation of what could come next was killing him.

Despite how things had ended, he found himself thinking about Anika; whether she would disregard him and tell Spence what they'd done. Spence had seemed quiet whenever Cameron saw him, but he figured this was due to Natty's troubles.

Cameron wasn't worried about Spence's reaction to finding out about him and Anika. If it came to it, he could easily eliminate his friend. Natty would be more of a challenge, though, and there wasn't a chance he wouldn't come after Cameron if anything happened to Spence. Despite this, he was comforted by the fact that he had backup — at least in the form of Wonder and Elijah. It put him in a strong position.

On a whim, Cameron found himself throwing on a designer tracksuit, using his expensive aftershave, and driving to Lorraine's one day. He'd spoken with Natty, and knew they were on the outs. He remembered how she had spurned him when they'd spoken at Ellie's party that time, and wondered how she would react now that Natty had almost killed her baby father.

Lorraine's mum opened the door to Cameron, frowning as she looked out at him. Cameron gave her a charming smile. She wasn't bad looking, he mused. She was shorter than her daughter, and a bit heavier, but she clearly took care of herself, and she had a pretty face.

'Can I help you?' She asked, unmoved by him.

'I . . . was hoping I could see Lorraine for a bit, just to see how she is. I'm Natty's boy,' he added, when the woman's expression remained unchanged. Without a word, she let him in.

Lorraine was on the sofa watching television. Despite knowing what Raider had done, Cameron was still startled when he saw the bruising on Lorraine's face. She smiled at him when she saw him.

'Do you need anything, Lo?' Her mum asked. Lorraine shook her head. 'I'll be in the kitchen.' With another look at Cameron, she left.

'How are you doing?' Cameron asked, when the door closed. Lorraine muted the television, wincing as she shifted. Cameron straightened up, ensuring his outfit and jewellery were clearly visible, but Lorraine's eyes locked onto his. They were a question, her brow furrowed in confusion.

'I've been better,' she said. 'There's a lot going on.'

'Yeah, I get that,' said Cameron. 'I spoke to Natty. He went too far with what he did.'

Lorraine shook her head. 'I don't want to talk about that, if you don't mind. Like I said, there's a lot going on.'

Cameron felt he was being dismissed, and he didn't like it.

Lorraine had to realise that things had changed now. Natty was the past. Cameron was the future.

'I get it. I mean, this shit's been brewing for a while. Especially after Natty flipped out on Wonder at that party that night, and then banged Ellie.' Cameron took pleasure when he saw Lorraine's face fall. He still had the video on his phone of them getting off, wondering if it would break Lorraine further if he showed her.

'You still had his back that night when he was about to fight Wonder and his friends, didn't you?' She finally replied.

'Course I did,' said Cameron. 'I always back my friends.'

'If that's the case, why are you here talking to me?'

Cameron was caught entirely off guard. Not only by the comment, but the palpable dislike in Lorraine's voice. He felt his anger grow, but held back.

'I thought you might need a friend, but it's cool. I'll leave you to it,' said Cameron. He expected Lorraine to stop him, but she didn't. As he left the house, he heard her mum re-enter the living room.

Cameron drove away, nostrils flaring at the disrespect. This wasn't how things were supposed to be now. He'd ascended. His friend had fallen. He deserved respect and adulation. Lorraine hadn't so much as looked at the clothes he'd worn or his jewellery. She simply wasn't interested, and that boiled Cameron's blood.

As he turned a corner, Cameron wondered how he'd got Anika so easily, but couldn't get Lorraine. Natty had messed up, but Lorraine still couldn't look past him. He had seen it in her face. No matter what was going on with Natty, she still cared for him.

Was this love?

Two days later, Rudy contacted Cameron, giving him a job. He and Wonder were told to go and shoot at a group of rival dealers in Harehills.

Wonder drove, and Cameron pulled on his leather gloves, not as nervous about the situation as he had been previously. He'd killed Christian. Shooting at some people he didn't know would be easy.

Wonder hadn't said much. Cameron had expected some talk about Rudy, and the potential plan to remove him, but Wonder had focused on business.

'These lot are nothing,' he said. 'They're lucky they're only getting a warning. Elijah thinks we can talk them into working for us without it getting bloody, though.'

'Why didn't he try talking to them first?'

Wonder chuckled, switching lanes. 'That stuff that happened with Warren a while back. Elijah and Natty tried talking to him, and Warren mugged them off. I think he's worried about the same thing happening again.'

Little more was said. Cameron took a deep breath as they approached the location. According to reports, the crew based out of a house on Darfield Street, which was full of terraced, red-bricked properties. The lights were on at the house, but no one was outside, which surprised Cameron. He'd expected them to have someone looking out, but it didn't matter.

The car window wound down, and he fired several shots at the house. He heard yells, but didn't stop, firing several more times, then firing a few shots at the upstairs windows for good measure.

Without being told, Wonder drove away at speed, tyres screeching as they took the corner. After a few minutes, they slowed down, Wonder giving Cameron a wide smile.

'You did good, bro. When the time comes, we know you're not gonna hold back.'

Cameron grinned. When the time came, he didn't intend to.

'We'll see what they do next. Elijah's gonna send someone to speak to them. If they don't play ball, we might have to go back. Do you have a problem with that?'

'No,' said Cameron. He still had the gun by his side, which was brave. He was ready to toss it if they saw police, though.

Soon, they dumped the car, getting into a second car driven by Marlon.

'Any trouble?' He asked the pair.

'Nah, Cam smashed it,' said Wonder. Marlon nodded at Cameron.

'Good work as always.'

Cameron preened, happy to be recognised for his work ethic. It seemed like just yesterday he was standing outside Maureen's, trying to get Marlon to take him seriously. He had come a long way, and it amazed him when he thought about it.

Cameron could do what he wanted, and the feeling was intense. He had disposable money and an assured position in the next big organisation. He no longer gambled in desperation, hoping to score quick winnings that he would rapidly blow. Now, gambling was about the thrill of the chase. The exhilaration of being right or wrong.

As he looked down at the watch on his wrist, he remembered the lengths he had gone to to get it. It was authentic; wearing fakes was a thing of the past. His mind drifted to Lodi, and Cameron frowned at the thought. He hadn't gone to bother Philip in a while, but wondered if he'd heard from Lodi since the last time.

'Everything okay?' Wonder was watching him.

'Yeah . . . I was just thinking about some old business. Do either of you two know Lodi?'

Marlon chuckled. 'Yeah. He's a character. I saw his girlfriend yesterday when I was doing some shopping. I don't know what she's doing messing with him. She could do a lot better.'

'I didn't even know he had a girlfriend,' said Cameron, feeling his excitement grow. A girlfriend meant he had roots. That meant that Cameron could get to him.

'They haven't been together all that long, but I'm pretty sure they live together.'

'I don't suppose you have the address, do you?'

'I could get hold of it,' said Marlon. 'Why?'

'Let's just say I've got some business to sort out with him.' Cameron grinned in anticipation of what he was going to do.

CHAPTER TWENTY-FIVE

CAMERON'S MIND whirred as he drove to the address he'd gotten from Marlon. He couldn't believe he was so close. Lodi had haunted Cameron since he'd managed to scam him. He had been hoodwinked, and he loathed the fact it made him feel inept and weak. It was holding him back, and he would finally have an opportunity to right the wrong.

Reaching the Garforth location and parking down the road, he had a good view of the house. After a while, he saw Lodi's girlfriend leaving. She was short and curvy, with blonde hair and pale eyes. She had a little acne on her forehead, but was still very pretty. Marlon was right about her being too good for Lodi, he mused. Still, she didn't matter. He hoped she didn't get in the way. All he wanted was Lodi.

An hour later, he sat up in the car. Lodi left the house, talking on a phone, looking as arrogant as ever. Cameron's fists clenched. He was ready to finish him off, but it was the middle of the day. He knew where he was staying now. He drove away, already planning to return later.

———

Rudy sipped tea, watching Tia eat her breakfast. Some mornings, she liked to eat light, and today she had a small selection of fruit, and a cup of coffee. Rudy enjoyed their peaceful mornings. There hadn't been as many lately. It felt like there was always a fire to put out, but for now, he just wanted to enjoy the moment.

'We've made some progress lately,' he said, still holding his cup. 'I think we're nearly ready to enact the plan.'

Tia looked up, her expression unreadable.

'What's going on with my son?'

Rudy sighed. He'd known this would come up.

'I hope he'll make the right decision when it all goes down,' he replied. 'Since he got sacked, he's kept a low profile, which is good. I thought he might fly off the handle and make a nuisance of himself.'

'Nat's stubborn,' said Tia. 'Always has been. You need to realise something, though. Something I don't think you want to accept.'

'What's that?' Rudy finally put down the cup, and finished the rest of his fried breakfast.

'If you take out his uncle, he will never follow you.'

Rudy looked at Tia thoughtfully.

'I hope you're wrong about that.'

Tia shook her head.

'I'm not wrong. I know you've always tried to have a relationship with Nat, but my son is a Dunn, and he's proud of his surname. You know what getting him to turn on Mitch will cost. Are you willing to pay the price?'

She returned to her food. Rudy stared at her, troubled by the remarks. Tia was right. Nathaniel was his father's son; a true Dunn. Sacrifices would have to be made if he wanted Natty on side.

Pushing his plate to the side, he considered if it was worth the risk.

Lodi left his house, smirking to himself. He was on his way to meet a group he'd been working on for a while. They thought they were investing into carefully selected stocks that would make them tons of profit, but they would be duped, and he would get their money. Approaching his car, he froze when a gun was pressed to his back.

'Mate, I don't know what this is about, but I've got a bit of money in my wallet, and you can take the car. Just let me go. Sound?'

'Walk back to the house. We're going inside.'

'I . . . listen—'

'I'll shoot you right here if you don't listen. Go. Now.'

Lodi didn't have a choice. Legs shaking, he headed back to his house, his hand trembling as he tried to unlock the door. He considered trying to surprise the gunman, but quickly gave up the idea. He wasn't a fighter. He was a talker. If the man felt more comfortable talking inside, he could go along with that. He was thankful Hannah wasn't home.

Lodi was pushed into the living room. When he turned and saw the stocky, angry-looking man for the first time, his mouth fell open in shock.

'You . . . you're *Connor*, right? Or is it *Curtis*? You're Phil's boy.'

'My name is Cam, dickhead. You ripped me off for five grand. It's taken me a while to track you down, but I've got you.'

Lodi's stomach plummeted. He remembered taking the money. He'd used it to take Hannah on holiday. Lodi had felt bad for Philip, but reasoned they weren't that close, anyway. He wondered how *Cam* had managed to track him down, but wasn't going to risk annoying him by asking.

'Cam . . . yeah, that's it. I remember you. I've been trying to find you myself. I got robbed after you gave me the money.

They worked me over pretty badly. I only recovered recently. I wanted to give you some money as good faith while I got the rest for you.'

'It's too late, you little shit,' said Cam, scowling. 'You mugged me off, and now you're gonna pay.'

'Please, Cam. I'm sorry. Let me make it right. I'm running something at the moment. I've got a final meeting with four dudes. They're going to give me the money. I'm talking over twenty grand. I'll split it with you.'

Cam hesitated, and Lodi felt relief surging through him. He was going for it. All he needed to do was pay off Cam, and then he could go about his business. Even if he lost out on his score, he could run another one later down the line. He couldn't do it if he was dead.

'I want whatever money you've got on you, as a show of good faith.'

Lodi nodded, feeling his heart rate returning to normal. He could do this. He just needed to keep it up for a while longer.

They went upstairs, Cam still carrying the gun. Lodi went to his bedroom, rooting around under the bed.

'Oi, don't try anything stupid,' said Cam. 'I'll blow your head off before you get the chance.'

'I won't. This is where my money is,' replied Lodi. He grabbed the handfuls of cash he had, putting them on the bed. 'There's around three grand there. I'll get the rest for you by the end of the day. Within two days tops. I promise.'

Cam smirked, and Lodi knew his whole world was about to come crashing down. He opened his mouth but didn't get the chance to speak as a bullet slammed into his stomach. He felt the burn as another shot smashed into his body. He was on the ground now, the world burning, his trousers wet as he relieved himself, unable to hold it in. Cam stalked closer, still holding the gun. His smirk widened, and then he pulled the trigger a third time, and Lodi knew no more.

HUSTLER'S AMBITION

———

CAMERON TURNED AWAY from Lodi and took a deep breath, trying to regulate his breathing. He looked around for a bag, finding one in a nearby wardrobe, stuffing the money into it, along with the gun. He headed from the house on shaky legs, ensuring his hood was up as he climbed into his car and drove away. Halfway home, he dumped the car on a street and walked away. It wasn't his, so he wasn't worried about it being traced back to him.

He took a moment to finally acknowledge what he'd done, as he brought up the Uber app on his phone. He had finally avenged the wrong. Lodi had taken advantage of him, and Cameron had handled him the right way, and had done so ruthlessly.

Noting that his driver was two minutes away, he grinned. He would relax for now, but he wondered whether he needed to eliminate Phil too.

When Cameron got home, he cleaned himself up, then made a drink, staring into space. He grabbed his phone and brought up Anika's number, staring at it for a moment. He'd been vicious when he'd cut her off. Pressing the call button, he frowned when it went straight to voicemail.

Breaking it off with her had seemed the right thing to do at the time. He hadn't wanted to go against Natty, and felt it was only a matter of time before they got caught. Now, he wondered if he should have kept her on the string for longer. As Cameron finished his drink and poured another, he was still pondering.

CHAPTER TWENTY-SIX

RUDY SAT in Delores's kitchen, awaiting Elijah and Wonder. He'd called them a while ago, asking them to be here. Marlon was currently unavailable, but Rudy planned to catch him up later.

When Elijah and Wonder appeared, they entered the room, a large man following closely behind. Rudy's eyes followed him as he stepped into the light.

'What's he doing here?' Rudy asked.

'He's here for protection,' said Elijah. 'Things are ramping up lately.'

'Send him to the other room or something. He doesn't need to be in here with us.'

'Wait in there,' Elijah said to the man, who nodded and left them. Rudy didn't like what he was seeing. He wondered if he was going to have problems with Elijah. There was tension developing between the pair, and Rudy had noticed a growing trend in his new partner. He was beginning to work more independently, consulting Rudy less. It was concerning.

Rudy made a mental note to strategise contingencies. If Elijah was going to prove a problem, it was one he would have to solve.

RICKY BLACK

For now, he would play along.

Rudy fetched drinks for everyone, and they spoke about bits of Hood gossip for a while. The pair had seemed on edge when they arrived, but had calmed down by now, meaning Rudy could get down to business.

'Did you handle the pickup?'

'Course I did,' replied Wonder. 'The Money is low. Second week running.'

'That's the *Natty effect*,' said Elijah, his mouth twisted, showing his distaste. 'Say what you want about him . . . He knew how to keep that team humming.'

'I'll get them in line. Don't worry about that,' said Wonder, snorting. 'Natty's not the only money-maker.'

Rudy almost smirked. Wonder was clearly jealous of Nathaniel. He wasn't even sure the little maggot realised it.

'Forget that,' He spoke now, thinking on his earlier words with Tia. 'Little London served its purpose, but we have other things to consider. Who should we use for the hit?'

'I'd have used Raider, if your stepson hadn't nearly killed him,' replied Elijah.

'I could do it,' said Wonder.

'Clearly, we need to think on this more, ' Rudy said. 'Mitch won't be easy to get.'

'Anyone can be taken out,' said Elijah. 'We've already gone over this. Our people won't wait forever.'

'We won't get a second chance. I've worked with him for decades. I know how he thinks.'

'You mean you've worked *for him*,' retorted Elijah.

'That doesn't matter. Remember why we're here. Why we're on the same page. I don't think you understand. If we miss this, we're fucked. No two ways about it. It needs to happen, so that means we have to be swift, and leave *no* room for failure.'

Before Elijah or Wonder could speak, they heard several bangs, and loud grunts. They rushed into the next room, to find Nathaniel standing over Elijah's bodyguard, breathing hard.

Rudy couldn't believe it. Nathaniel was there. He'd stumbled onto their meeting. His stomach plummeted, and he made his decision in an instant.

'He heard everything. Kill him.'

Nathaniel didn't hesitate, turning and running as several wild shots missed him.

'Go! Get him!' Rudy yelled. Grumbling, Wonder dragged the bodyguard to his feet, and they went after Nathaniel.

'What now?' Elijah asked, his voice panicked. He too, knew what Nathaniel getting away would mean.

'Now, we wait. He needs to die.'

Elijah shook his head.

'If we'd killed him when we had the chance, then none of this would have happened.'

'That doesn't matter now,' snapped Rudy, wiping his face. 'I explained why we couldn't kill him. I'm not going to do so again.'

Elijah grumbled, but said nothing.

―――

Before long, Wonder and the bodyguard returned, both out of breath.

'We lost him,' said Wonder. Rudy turned away for a moment, gritting his teeth. When it was clear his anger wasn't waning, he went off.

'You fucking idiot,' he snarled. 'How the hell did you let him get away? You both had fucking guns, you imbecile. You should have shot him.'

'Don't fucking blame me,' Wonder snapped back. 'All of this is your fault, coming up with your shitty, complicated plan.'

'You dare speak to me like that?' Rudy didn't care

anymore. He wasn't bothered how important Wonder was to Elijah. He would die for his disrespect.

'Look, this isn't the time,' Elijah interjected. 'We need to move, or we're fucked. We need to activate whatever men we've got on the inside, and start this war right now. Even if we don't get Mitch, we can cripple his power base, and smoke him out.'

Before Rudy could respond, his phone rang.

'What?' He snapped, seeing Cameron's number. He didn't have time for his nonsense right now.

'Natty's here,' Cameron said, talking quietly. 'He knows about the plan. Says you lot tried killing him.'

Rudy's lips curled into a menacing smile as relief washed over him. They had Nathaniel right where they wanted him. Their plan was still in play.

'Keep him there. I'm sending some people to handle it right now. Well done.' Rudy hung up, facing the group. 'He's at Cameron's house. I'll give you the address. Go over there, finish him, and don't mess up this time.'

Wonder nodded his head in response and turned to leave.

'Wonder.'

He paused, looking over his shoulder at Rudy.

'This is a tricky situation for Cameron. He's shown great loyalty in calling this in. But if you get the faintest impression he is going to turn on us, you shoot him without hesitation. Do you understand?'

Again, Wonder nodded, turning the door handle and exiting the house, a small smile on his face.

CHAPTER TWENTY-SEVEN

CAMERON PUT his phone in his pocket, pleased he'd acted so quickly when Natty turned up. He'd been drinking the night away when Natty had burst in, and had thought the game was up. Luckily, Natty hadn't known he was involved.

Everything was in play now. They would need to kill Natty, and then make their move. Rudy had been too cautious, and now everything was in danger of unravelling. He would need to speak with Wonder as soon as possible, and find out their next step.

Grabbing the gun he'd used on Lodi, Cameron headed back into the living room, stopping short when he heard Natty speaking to Spence. Knowing he'd messed up, there was only one thing to do.

'Hang up.'

Natty turned, freezing when he saw Cameron pointing the gun at him.

'Why, Cam?' Natty said, after a moment's silence. He sounded so crushed, that Cameron nearly laughed. *Big, bad Natty*, had been caught out, and he knew it.

'You're not the only one who has plans. Big things are happening. I was smart enough to get in on the ground floor.'

Natty shook his head, seeming to deflate before Cameron's eyes.

'I may have had plans, but you were always with me, fam. I'd have taken you wherever I went, and you know that.'

'Don't give me that crap!' Cameron exploded. He had no intention of listening to Natty try to talk his way out of this. He was no better than Lodi. 'All you care about is yourself. You didn't bring me into Little London to get money with you. You put Spence in charge over me, and just expected me to take it. When did you ever do anything for me?'

Natty's brow furrowed. He looked less worried now, and Cameron's finger tightened around the gun.

'Who turned you? Elijah? Rudy? One of the flunkies?'

'Does it matter? You're finished either way. Your uncle can't survive what's going on. He'd never have gotten as far as he did without Rudy.'

'Is Spence involved?'

Cameron scoffed. That showed just how pathetic Natty's thinking was. *He didn't have a clue.*

'Spence is as soft as you. You're both pussy whipped, especially you. You should have died for the beating you gave Raider. Truthfully, Elijah pushed for that, but Rudy talked him out of it.'

'How long have you hated me?'

'I don't hate you.' Cameron's mouth fell open a moment. For a moment, he remembered the pair as kids, sitting in the park, planning their futures. Then he smiled, pushing away those useless memories. 'You're just weak. The moves you've made have been trash. You're a little bitch for your uncle, and he's a damn coward. Too scared to even show his face in public.'

'What happens next?' Natty asked calmly.

'I called Rudy. Men are on their way to take care of you.'

Natty smirked. Cameron's grin vanished. He didn't know why Natty looked so pleased. It made him want to smash the gun into his face, until the smug, superior look left it.

'Why are you smiling? Did you hear what I said?'

'No matter what team you're on, you end up as the bitch, don't you? Whether it's me, or Elijah, or Rudy, no one respects you. We use you for the little things,' said Natty.

Cameron stepped forward, his anger growing. *Natty was wrong. Cameron was a force. He was ruthless. Unlike Natty, he'd killed people.*

'I'm a big part of the plan. For once, you're not the main guy, and you can't deal with it,' he finally said. Natty laughed, which only made Cameron more flustered.

'I'll die knowing I'm not a boot licker like you, Cam. People only respect you because of me, and deep down, you know that. I bet that's how they got to you. I'll tell you this, though: first chance they get, you'll be out, because, without me, you're nothing.'

Cameron's finger tightened on the trigger. Natty was pushing it. *If Rudy was sending people to the house anyway, what did it matter who did the job?*

'Are you even *allowed* to kill me?' Natty laughed. 'We keep our instructions simple with you, so you don't fuck them up. It's part of your programming.'

'You lost, Natty. I could take you if I wanted to. I don't take orders from anyone,' snapped Cameron, trembling with rage when he saw Natty grinning. Natty wasn't better than him. They both knew it.

'You still need to wait for backup, right? You ran to call as soon as I got here. Didn't have the guts to take me on without a gun, right? And you have the nerve to call me and Spence pussies?'

That was it. He would deal with Rudy and everyone else later. This was his last test. When he took out Natty, no one could say he wasn't his own man again. Putting down the gun, he kicked it away. With a yell, he charged Natty, who didn't move, allowing himself to be taken to the floor. They wrestled around, Natty quickly getting the momentum.

Cameron was no slouch, and knew how to fight, but Natty was bigger and more scientific. In his rage, Cameron had forgotten that. Natty landed several solid punches to Cameron's chest and stomach, each leaving Cameron feeling like he'd been hit with a cannonball. Natty wrapped his arm around Cameron's throat and squeezed. Cameron kicked, trying to break the grip, but Natty had the move locked in, feeling his movements growing weaker.

Heavy footsteps distracted Natty, causing him to loosen the hold. Cameron took advantage, elbowing him several times and breaking free just as Spence burst in, aiming a gun at Cameron. Cameron's heart leapt in his throat, but then Wonder and another man burst in, also with guns. Cameron grinned. The cavalry was here to rescue him.

'I was wondering when you guys—'

The rest of his words were cut off when Wonder shot him in the shoulder. Cameron toppled to the ground with a yelp, cradling his bleeding arm. In that instant, he knew he'd made a terrible mistake.

CHAPTER TWENTY-EIGHT

RUDY HAD his phone in hand. He'd already made two phone calls, trying to keep track of what was going on. He'd heard nothing from Wonder, who wasn't answering. There was the chance something had gone wrong, and he needed to make the right moves, but seeing Natty had thrown him off.

Wonder had been given a simple directive; go to Cameron's, and take out Natty. The house wasn't far away. He should have been back by now.

Elijah was pacing the room, increasingly annoyed every time he saw Rudy lower the phone.

'What are we going to—'

A loud bang distracted them, four men charging into the kitchen. Rudy and Elijah had no chance. They were taken down and zip-tied before they could even blink. Taken from the house without a word, the kitchen was left empty, chairs toppled and glasses broken.

CAMERON WAS STILL IN A DAZE, his shoulder feeling like it was on fire. Several more men had entered his house, and they had disarmed Wonder and the man he'd brought with him. Cameron was then roughly dragged to his feet, and his hands were zip-tied behind his back. It put tremendous pressure on his injured shoulder, causing him to scream, but no one paid any attention.

Cameron was shoved into the back of a white van. Panic growing, he realised he needed to do something. Anything.

'Oi, you pieces of shit,' he shouted, as the van drove away. 'Do you know who the fuck I am? You better let me out of here, or it's gonna be bad!'

He received no response, despite trying several other threats. By the time the van stopped, and the doors opened, he was ready to bargain.

'Look, I was forced to be involved,' he said. 'Natty is my best friend. They threatened me, but I'd never have done anything to harm him. He's like my brother.'

Cameron's words fell on deaf ears. He was led inside a house, and placed on a chair in a windowless room. He shouted for someone to listen, but there was no response. He lost track of how long he had been in the room when the light was suddenly switched on. He watched a woman dragging a stool along, which she sat on, facing him.

Despite the pain in his arm, and the uncertainty of the situation, Cameron was blown away by how beautiful the woman was. She was slender, with dark hair, alluring eyes, and an overall sexual demeanour. Despite himself, he stared at her.

'Hello, Cameron.' Her voice was as soft as he imagined, and he savoured each word.

'Hi . . .' he replied, still trying to work out what was going on.

'What do you have to tell me?' The woman asked.

'I don't know what's going on. I was for—'

'You're lying.'

'I'm not. I—'

'We know, Cameron. Everything. We knew even before we caught your friend, Marlon, trying to get words to his contacts. He's dead, by the way.'

Cameron felt dizzy. His head lolling forward, overwhelmed by the moment. He didn't know who the woman was, but there had been no hesitation when she had spoken of killing. The fact she also knew who Marlon was, was telling.

'If you don't want to go the same, excruciating way as Marlon, I suggest you start talking.'

Cameron glared at the woman, not liking how she was speaking to him, the anger overruling the overwhelming fear for a second.

'Your shoulder must be hurting,' the woman said. 'A gunshot is nothing to play around with. I should add that if I don't get a response, then in exactly sixty seconds, I'm going to get my tools and get to work. *Fifty-seven. . . fifty-six. . . fifty-five. . .*'

Cameron tried to hold out, but by the time she'd counted down to thirty, he broke, telling her of Rudy and Marlon bringing him on board, and the connection to Elijah and Wonder. When he finished speaking, she shot him a dazzling smile that, despite the situation, Cameron reacted to, smiling back. His smile vanished when a man entered the room and handed the woman a knife. She slid to her feet, her movements fluid as she stalked toward him.

Frantically, Cameron tried to break free, but it was to no avail. Her hand was a blur. There was a split-second of overwhelming pain, and then darkness.

———

CLARKE ENTERED the room where Wonder waited. He hadn't resisted them. Once they'd entered Cameron's, he'd known the game was up, and had fully cooperated. Clarke surveyed him for a long moment, noting his deflated demeanour. It was hard to believe he'd been an integral part of an attempt to kill his boss.

Still, that didn't matter now.

'Everyone involved in the attempt against my boss has been taken care of,' he said. 'Everyone but you.'

Wonder trembled, tears spilling down his cheeks as he cried. Clarke felt nothing for him, and let him continue for a few moments.

'We're willing to let you live.'

Cautiously, Wonder stared up at Clarke, as if he didn't believe him.

'Why would you do that?' He croaked. Clarke smiled.

'In case we've missed anybody. You'll be able to tell people how stupid it is to think you can get the drop on us. You can lead the few people in your ragtag crew that weren't involved in your ridiculous plan.'

'I . . . I'll do it,' said Wonder. He'd have done anything to stay alive, unable to keep the relief from his voice.

'Okay. We're going to let you go. You're going to go home, and await our people calling on you later. You're not going to tell anyone what's going on. You're not going to attempt to run. Not only will we catch you, we'd be forced to make an example out of you, which would likely include something bad happening to your sick nana. Am I understood?'

Shaking, Wonder nodded.

'Excellent. One last thing . . . there won't be another chance.'

———

SPENCE AND NATTY sat outside Natty's house, waiting for Clarke to arrive. He'd called them both, requesting to speak.

The friends hadn't spoken much, still trying to process the situation. Cameron had turned on them, and they had both nearly died. On top of everything else that had recently transpired, it was a lot to take in.

By the time Clarke arrived, they were relieved, grateful for the momentary distraction.

They went inside, everyone remaining standing.

'I wanted to tell you both face to face that the issue has been fully rectified. Everyone who was involved, has been taken care of. Natty, your uncle will be in touch in the near future to speak to you. Spence, you're in charge for now. Do either of you have any questions?'

Spence opened his mouth, ready to ask about Cameron. He had betrayed them, but he still wanted to know his fate. As he stared at Clarke, though, he found he couldn't ask. He glanced at Natty, who was looking at the floor, then back to Clarke, whose eyes hadn't left him.

Finally, he shook his head.

'No, I don't have any questions.'

'Good. Sit tight, boys. Big changes are on the horizon for us all.'

DID YOU ENJOY THE READ?

Thank you for reading Hustler's Ambition!

It was always my intent to write a short story about Cameron and his motives, and the concept grew wings, as these things often do!

Please take a minute or two to help me by leaving a review – even if it's just a few lines. Reviews help massively with getting my books in front of new readers. I personally read every review and take all feedback on board.

To support me, please click the relevant link below:
　　UK: http://www.amazon.co.uk/review/create-review?&asin=B0B7JZXF2J

US: http://www.amazon.com/review/create-review?&asin=B0B7JZXF2J

Make sure you're following me on Amazon to keep up to date with my releases, or that you're signed up to my email list, and I'll see you at the next book!

READ BLOOD AND BUSINESS

Tyrone Dunn wants to take over Leeds, and he is willing to battle anyone who gets in his way.

Even family.

Will it be settled by blood . . . or business?

Order now, and find out.

ALSO BY RICKY BLACK

The Target Series:

Origins: The Road To Power

Target

Target Part 2: The Takedown

Target Part 3: Absolute Power

The Complete Target Series Boxset

The Deeds Family Series:

Blood & Business

Good Deeds, Bad Deeds

Deeds to the City

Hustler's Ambition

No More Deeds (TBC)

Other books by Ricky Black:

Homecoming

ABOUT RICKY BLACK

Ricky Black was born and raised in Chapeltown, Leeds.

In 2016, he published the first of his crime series, Target, and has published ten more books since.

Visit https://rickyblackbooks.com for information regarding new releases and special offers, and promotions.

Copyright © 2023 by Ricky Black

All rights reserved.

No part of this book may be reproduced in any form or by any electronic or mechanical means, including information storage and retrieval systems, without written permission from the author, except for the use of brief quotations in a book review.

Printed in Great Britain
by Amazon